One More Round

One More Round

A McLaughlin Romance

Shelli Stevens

TULE
PUBLISHING

Dedication

A huge thank you and virtual hug to my readers, and to Tule publishing for giving this story a new home. I hope you enjoy this story as much as I do! Thanks again to 'Becca from the beach for your help with legalese. To my friends at The Owl N' Thistle (and Fadó) for your bartending and bar info! And always, to my family and friends who rally around me with support. I'd especially love to thank Bill—once just a friend now husband—who let me steal the McLaughlin name for my book series and for being so supportive of me over the years.

Chapter One

SARAH RAWLINGS GRIPPED the cool railing of the ferry-
boat and sucked in a deep breath.

Salty air that she could almost taste coated her throat.
Somehow it managed to be both warm and crisp. Invigorat-
ing. Alive. It was early summer in the Pacific Northwest, and
God she'd forgotten how much she loved the season here.

Opening her eyes, she slid her gaze out over the blue
skies that had a few fluffy white clouds strewn about almost
as an afterthought.

The slight rise and fall of the ferry gliding over the waves
of Puget Sound matched the churning in her stomach.

She glanced out toward the island they approached.
There were more houses now scattered along the cliffs. They
seemed bigger, fancier, but the south end of the island still
looked familiar. Beautiful and rich with its abundance of
evergreen trees.

Had it really been eleven years since she'd lived on
Whidbey? It didn't seem like that much time had passed.
That she'd only had the privilege of calling this island home

for eight years of her life.

But that was the life of a navy brat. Don't get attached to any place, to anyone, because the rug only stayed under your feet for so long.

Leaving Whidbey, though, had been the hardest move she'd ever made over the years by far. And now, for the first time since she'd left, she was coming back.

It wasn't the light wind that sent chills through her body and lifted the hairs on her arms, but the knowledge of what she was returning to. Or more so, who.

Her heart quickened and she tightened her fingers on the railing until her knuckles went white.

No. If all goes right, you'll be on and off this island quickly enough without ever having to see him.

Her phone buzzed in her pocket. Grateful for the distraction from her thoughts, Sarah plucked it free and read the message from Kenzie.

> I see the ferry you're on! You should be here any minute. Just walk off the boat and I'll be in the parking lot waiting. Holy shitballs, I am SO excited to see you!!!

Laughing softly, she typed a quick reply in acknowledgment, not having to feign excitement.

She was excited—really she was. She hadn't seen Kenzie in over a decade and they'd been best friends while Sarah lived on the island. Even after she'd left, they'd kept in touch through email and social media.

It was the possibility of seeing other people that worried

her. The fear of ripping scabs off wounds that had never healed. It was that latter possibility that made the breakfast sandwich she'd eaten ten minutes ago threaten to come right back up.

Knowing that soon they'd land at the small ferry dock, Sarah grabbed her suitcase that rested next to her and made her way downstairs.

Once she was standing at the front of the boat, securely tucked behind the safety rope, she again drank in the sight of the island they were almost upon.

As they grew closer, her pulse seemed to get a little more erratic. Her palms damp.

Maybe I shouldn't have come. But no. She'd already made too many mistakes in her life—this wouldn't be another one.

She turned her gaze to the dark churning waters of Puget Sound. White foam sprayed frantically into the air as the boat cut through the water.

Next to her was another group of walk-on passengers. There were a couple of bicyclists, and a family with a little girl who looked preschool age. The little girl squealed with excitement as she pointed at the waves and the flurry of bubbles around the moving boat.

A lump settled in Sarah's throat as she watched the girl, and tears pricked at the backs of her eyes. Guilt stabbed briefly in her heart but she pushed it aside.

Emily's fine. You know she is. Skip the guilt and focus on the task ahead, missy.

She kept that mantra in her head until the ferry had docked and she was striding off it to find Kenzie.

It didn't take long to spot the braided strawberry blonde in the Aerosmith T-shirt, waving her arms above her head like a fool.

"Holy shit," Kenzie squealed, launching away from her car and running to hug her. "I can't believe you're really here."

Sarah embraced her friend, laughing with ease now as the tension slipped away.

Oh God, she hadn't even realized how much she missed this girl. It had been a decade, but some friendships didn't feel time. This was one of them.

Kenzie pulled back, her eyes shiny with tears. "How are we just a couple years from thirty? You have so few pictures on Facebook, but you look exactly the same as you did back then. Wait, no, you're even hotter than you were in high school."

"Am I?" Sarah laughed and shrugged. "I'm a single mom now, so I suppose I need to try harder to impress the opposite sex if I ever want to meet someone."

"Oh hell, I hear you on that." Kenzie scowled. "Not the single mom bit, but the trying to impress guys bit."

"Seriously? How are *you* still single?" Sarah pulled away and ran a glance over her friend.

"Well, it's like my family says: I must have high standards."

And Kenzie always had. Her friend hadn't changed much over the years either. Still skinny enough to make other women envious, and with the same set of boobs that had never failed to trip up the football players when the girls had been cheerleading at a game.

Add to that, she was a *McLaughlin*. The entire family was legend on the island and had been hugely popular since they'd moved to the States from Scotland fifteen or so years ago.

Kenzie, the youngest and only girl out of the four kids, had been in America so long she'd lost most of her accent. But any guy she met had always seemed to seek her attention. Just like the females on the island had all been starry-eyed for her three brothers.

Just thinking back to those days when she and Kenzie had been a little wild—and a lot naïve—had Sarah's heart squeezing so hard she could barely draw in a breath.

"Okay, let's put your suitcase in the trunk and we'll head out." Kenzie grabbed Sarah's suitcase, ignoring her protests that she could put it in the trunk herself.

Minutes later they were settled into the Ford Escort and driving up the hill that led them into the heart of the island.

Sarah drank in every sight, noting the changes in businesses since the last time she'd been here. Some shops had been replaced. Some were out of business. And there were now some more commercial restaurants and various shops.

It was different, but it was still familiar. It was the island she'd spent eight years of her life on.

"So where is Emily? You didn't want to bring her?" Kenzie cast her an accusing glance. "I still have no idea what she looks like. You've never posted pics of her on Facebook."

"I'm not a fan of putting her picture online," Sarah admitted, keeping her gaze focused out the passenger window. "I'm all right being online, but I don't want my kid to be. I'll show you a picture of her later."

"Deal. Damn, I'm so glad you're back." Kenzie sighed. "Though the circumstances that brought you here aren't all that great. I was sorry to hear about your grandmother's passing."

"Thank you." Again she was stabbed by guilt, but this time she knew she deserved it.

Her grandma, who'd been recently widowed, had moved to Whidbey to be closer to Sarah's mom when the family had been stationed in Oak Harbor.

Only Grandma had stayed when Sarah's dad had gotten stationed in Japan and moved the entire family. Gran had fallen in love with the island and had decided it would be a nice place to retire.

And you never tried to visit her until it was too late. The devastating stroke that had taken her grandmother's life had been a shock to everyone. Sarah had kept telling herself she had time to visit some day when she was ready. But now that day had come, and unfortunately Gran was gone.

"You'll have to give me directions on where to turn. She

lived in Coupeville, right?"

"Right." Sarah stared at the blur of green from all the trees whizzing by.

"Cool, that's just over a half hour or so."

"I forgot how long this island is."

It was pretty big—something like the fourth longest island in the contiguous United States, if she remembered correctly.

She and her parents hadn't lived in Coupeville, though, but on the north end of the island up in Oak Harbor near the navy base.

"It's pretty big," Kenzie agreed. "Which makes it a bitch when you need to drive from Oak Harbor to catch the ferry. But then—what the...*crap*."

"What?" But even as Sarah asked, she realized what had happened.

The car began to slow in jerky spurts, and the *thud, thud, thud* came from what sounded like a flat tire.

Kenzie maneuvered the car to the side of the road and put it in park. She glanced over at Sarah and winced.

"Umm..."

"Flat tire? I've got this." Sarah reached for her seat belt. "My dad made sure I knew how to change one before I even got my license."

"That's not it. I know how to change a tire too." Kenzie tugged on a braid and grimaced. "It's just I was going on a camping trip a few weeks ago and wanted a little extra space—"

"You took out the spare?" Sarah guessed.

"I took out the spare."

Some things never changed. Fighting the urge to laugh or groan in frustration, Sarah just shrugged.

"Do you have AAA? We can get them out here—"

"No need. I've got brothers." Kenzie waved her hand, already dialing a number on her cell phone.

She was calling her brother? Gripping the seat belt now, Sarah's stomach went into full-on butter churn mode.

She couldn't face him. Couldn't see him.

"Kenzie…" Her plea was almost inaudible, but her friend must've heard it—and the sudden anxiety in her voice— because she glanced over quickly.

Sympathy flashed in her eyes. "Hey, don't sweat it. I'm calling Aleck."

Aleck. The oldest McLaughlin brother. Relief came immediately and filtered through her taut muscles. She managed a weak nod before resting her head back against the seat.

She couldn't focus on the conversation Kenzie was having. Couldn't do anything but try and get her heart rate back to normal.

What a stupid, ridiculous overreaction. What the hell was wrong with her?

"Help is on the way." Kenzie set her phone down in her lap and sighed. After a moment, she glanced at Sarah. "You know I wouldn't do that to you. I wouldn't throw you into an awkward situation with Ian. It's not my business, and you need to face those demons when you're ready."

She'd be ready about a quarter after never. Wasn't going to happen. Couldn't happen. But, dammit, she'd known that just being on the island was gambling with the fact it *might* happen.

"I'm only here for a short while." Sarah hesitated, trying to figure out how to put it delicately. "No offense, but you're the only McLaughlin I intended to spend time with."

A flicker of sadness passed over her friend's face, but she nodded. "Understandable. Sorry I threw a wrench in those plans by making Aleck bring me a spare."

"It's fine. Really." She could handle Aleck. He'd always been sweet and funny. Very much like the big brother she'd never had but wouldn't have minded having.

Kenzie nodded. "Okay. So tell me about Virginia. How do you like living there?"

Appreciating the change of subject, Sarah told her about what had brought her there and how living across the country was. She'd begun to relax again, to enjoy the conversation with her old friend, when Kenzie whipped around and stared out the rear window.

"Son of a *bitch*."

"What is it?" Sarah turned to follow her gaze.

The red Camaro that roared up behind Kenzie's car stopped maybe a foot from them, close enough to make her think he'd nudge their bumper.

That car. She knew that car.

Her heart, which she'd managed to slow, picked right back up again.

Please no.

"Can't anybody follow instructions?" Kenzie growled, and opened her door. "Stay in here, Sarah. I'll handle this."

This wasn't happening. Sarah shook her head as the Camaro door opened and six feet of tall, hard male slid out.

Everything inside her head started to spin as he strode toward Kenzie, a big, shit-eating grin on his face.

Sarah gripped the edge of her seat, her nails digging into the fabric. Her neck started to protest the awkward, twisted position, but she couldn't look away.

Shock cocooned her body, but through it, almost clinically, she drank him in. He looked so much like he had eleven years ago. Beneath the tinted sunglasses she knew she'd find those rare, piercing green eyes all the McLaughlins had.

His brown hair held a hint red in the sunlight, and it was just a little too long. The body, still tall and solid, was maybe even bigger now. It looked as if he'd taken up lifting weights.

His shoulders were wide and she couldn't help but remember how she used to cling to them when his mouth was on hers. How those shoulders, and his hands on her waist, had been the only things that kept her standing.

Just like all the McLaughlin boys, he was entirely too

sexy. But more than sexy, he seemed dangerous. Especially now. He was the ultimate bad boy, seemed happy to claim the title and revel in it.

Instinct demanded she run. That she jump out of the car and run like a startled deer into the woods, no matter how illogical and ridiculous it seemed.

Whatever Kenzie was yelling at her brother couldn't reach her ears through the car, but the tone did. Kenzie was livid.

Her brother shook his head, and then his big grin vanished. He yanked off his sunglasses and whipped his gaze to the car to where Sarah sat in frozen disbelief.

Their gazes locked and her world bottomed out.

It was unavoidable. She would have to face him. The realization that she had no choice became evident when Ian ignored his sister's protests and strode toward the car.

No, no, no.

Despite the childish instinct to hit the lock and keep him out, she made no effort to stop him when he reached her door and pulled it open.

"As I live and breathe. Sarah Thornton." His Scottish accent was faint, but stronger than his sister's. The voice was so familiar and had the power to make her knees weaken.

But even though he smiled, his eyes were frigid emerald stones that pierced deep. They were potent enough to shatter her heart all over again.

He tilted his head and murmured, "Welcome back to

Whidbey Island."

IAN MADE SURE the shock riding through his system wasn't evident on his face. He draped an arm on the open door and stared down at her.

Sarah was here. On the island. Fuck it all.

How long had it been? A decade? No, more. Eleven years, almost exactly.

Eleven years since she'd up and left without so much as a good-bye.

As a teenager she'd been pretty. He knew her exotic looks came partly from her grandmother, who had come from India to marry an American soldier. Sarah had silky, black hair that had almost reached her waist—God he'd loved to touch that hair. And her flawless skin with a hint of olive that he'd spent so much time kissing. But then there were her eyes. Cloudy, blue pools of emotion that had never failed to make him trip over his tongue a little. And he wasn't the type to stutter.

Her body back then had been petite and thin, with just a bit of curve. But now… She was still thin, but not quite as skinny. A quick glance at the pink T-shirt she wore showed breasts that seemed fuller. The blood in his body pounded a little harder, because those tits had already been pretty damn amazing before. To think of that—

"Rawlings."

Jerking his mind off the dirty road it had wandered down, he arched a brow at the thread of hostility in her tone.

"What's that you say, doll?"

"It's Sarah Rawlings now."

The memory of how amazing her breasts had felt in his hands—not to mention his mouth—disappeared as her words penetrated.

"That's right." He gave a slow nod, not happy with the stab of something dark inside him. "I heard you got married. Had a kid."

"I did. But then, that's what responsible people do when they grow up. They settle down, maybe have a family." Her tone was indicative of someone talking to a child, and her smile was just condescending enough to make his teeth snap together.

"Aye? And how's that working out for you?" The taunting words were out before he could stop them.

Her eyes went wide, shock and hurt reflecting in their depths, before she seemed to school her expression again. Her delicate shoulders lifted in a stiff shrug.

"It didn't." She slid her gaze away from him and stared out the windshield. "I'm divorced now."

"Hey." Kenzie appeared at his side, tugging on his shirtsleeve. "You know I love you—there's nothing I wouldn't do for you, Ian. But you're being a total arse, so leave her alone already."

"Just getting reacquainted," he drawled and pulled his

arm off the door. "Now, you said something about a tire needing changing?"

The minute his arm was off the door, Sarah jerked it closed and he couldn't stop a chuckle when the lock clicked.

Almost as if she were afraid of him. He couldn't really blame her. Maybe he was being a bit of a bastard.

Kenzie glared at him, hands on her hips. "Are you daft? I specifically asked Aleck to come help me, not you."

"And he fully intended to come help you, until Old Man Cooper picked a fight with a sailor. I wasn't busy, so he asked me if I'd mind coming to your rescue."

His sister sighed, but the fury in her gaze diminished some and she gave a terse nod.

Because she bartended at the pub, she knew exactly who Dwayne Cooper was. A bit loud, but usually harmless, the elderly man was a regular at McLaughlin's Pub. He loved to boast of his Scottish roots—especially when he'd been drinking—and would engage anyone willing in a verbal debate over anything and everything. The man seemed to think he was twenty-five, not seventy-five.

"You should've sent Colin then." She mentioned Ian's twin brother's name with a grumpy tone that indicated she still wasn't pleased.

"The man is busy being a sheriff's deputy." Ian moved past her to his car, and plucked a tire from the back seat. "Besides, why are you so worried about Sarah and I running in to each other? We're both grown adults."

Kenzie snorted, folding her arms across her chest. "You think so, do you? Is that why you had to throw that taunt in her face about her marriage failing?"

Her words hit home, evoking guilt, but he didn't respond. Instead, he moved past her to return to her car and begin changing her tire.

"I know things didn't end well for you guys." She stayed on his heels, the move so familiar from when they'd been growing up.

Though instead of begging for sweets or money as she had when she was a child, now she scolded him.

"But you don't need to be a complete arse to her."

"Just a partial one?"

Kenzie whacked him on the shoulder. "You, big brother, are impossible. Change my tire and be gone already."

It should've been that easy, really. He should've wanted to be out of here as soon as possible. But as he snuck a glance at Sarah, hunkered down in the front seat as if hoping he'd forget she was there, he realized rushing away was the last thing on his mind.

"You'll have to ask Sarah to step out of the car while I do."

After a moment's silence, he glanced at his sister. Her expression held disbelief and frustration.

"Surely you can change a tire with her in the car. This is a busy road. She's tiny—barely five feet and probably a hundred and fifteen pounds soaking wet. There's no reason for her to get out of the car."

"There's no reason for her not to." He cocked his head. "Now, if you want me to change your tire, you'll have to move your friend."

Her eyes flashed, but for once she didn't argue and instead moved to go ask Sarah to get out of the car.

Even though he was rifling through the trunk of Kenzie's car, he caught the movement of Sarah exiting.

He slammed the trunk and straightened, jack in hand. He glanced over at the women, witty comment at the ready, but it died on his tongue.

Chapter Two

SARAH WAS TALKING quietly to Kenzie, her body twisted away from him. But the angle gave him a full view of all the curves she hadn't had the last time he'd seen her.

Sure she'd been pretty, but her looks had only been part of the reason he'd fallen for her. Her unwavering faith in him, and her ability to see beneath the surface of the image he projected, had struck him core deep.

Shoving all that bullshit aside—because it seemed it had been nothing more than illusion—she was a knockout now. Not overweight by any means, but she had more meat on her than before. Hips and an arse that definitely curved beneath dark jeans.

Mentally, he peeled off the clothes, imagining the body he'd once known with the new curves. What would it be like to explore them? To hold those sweet hips while driving into her—

Dammit, what the *hell* was he doing? He was not fantasizing about Sarah. That was a part of his life best buried and forgotten. They weren't two reckless teenagers anymore who acted on hormones and had silly visions of love. He'd moved on to other women, and Sarah...she had a kid. The last damn thing he wanted was to get involved with a single mom.

Children tended to fear him, and he returned the emotion somewhat. They were emotional, asked too many questions, and could be entirely too prone to leaky diapers and projectile vomit.

Scowling now, Ian turned away from the two and got started on changing Kenzie's tire.

By the time he'd finished, he was ready to get the hell out of Dodge.

Kenzie still glared at him—which was a bit ridiculous since he'd taken time out of his day off to help her—but Sarah still avoided looking at him completely.

Grabbing the flat tire, he placed it back in the trunk along with the jack and then turned to the women.

"That should do you, li'l sis."

She flashed him a hard, sarcastic smile. "Thanks. I appreciate your help. Best be on your way now, I'm sure—"

"So how long are you staying on the island?" He wiped the dirt and oil from his hands onto his jeans and glanced at Sarah.

She didn't answer right away, and he saw her chest slowly rise and fall and she seemed to take a deliberate breath in. Then she finally looked at him.

"Not too long. I'm only here to clean up Gran's house

and put it on the market."

Sarah had always been close to her grandma, and it must've been painful for her to deal with the loss. Had she ever visited? As far as he knew, Sarah hadn't returned to the island in the past eleven years. Word would've gotten out if she had.

"I was sorry to hear about Libby. I always liked her."

For a moment, tears brightened Sarah's blue eyes. She gave a jerky nod and looked down.

"Thank you. She liked you too." The words seemed almost reluctant. "Her death was a shock to everyone."

"I imagine so. I'm sure you're regretting not visiting her more often before she passed. Actually, now that I think about it, did you ever visit?"

There was such blatant pain and guilt in Sarah's eyes, for a moment, he would've sworn she was going to burst into tears.

But then she straightened her spine and she muttered, "You haven't changed a bit, have you, Ian? Still a complete jerk when you want to be."

"When I need to be," he agreed softly.

Kenzie stepped forward, placing herself between him and Sarah. "Okay, really? Stop this shit. What are you guys, fifteen?"

"Twenty-nine. Colin and I both are, actually. Twins if you recall."

"You're not even a little bit funny right now. In fact,

you're quickly making it on my shit list. So, yeah, we're going to leave." Kenzie's tone was overly bright for the heavy tension. "Thanks again for the tire."

Taking the not-so-subtle hint, Ian nodded and turned to walk back to his car.

"Good to see you again, Sarah." But it hadn't been. Not really. Seeing her had ripped open a wound he resented— one that shouldn't have existed.

As far as he was concerned, Sarah's presence on the island was completely unwelcome.

She didn't reply to his farewell, but then, he hadn't expected her to.

The sooner she left, the better.

∽

SILENCE WAS GOLDEN. Or it was the breeding ground for a host of memories and thoughts that were pure toxic.

Sarah locked the front door of her grandma's house and then pulled back the curtain on the window beside it.

She watched Kenzie's car speed off down the dirt road and could only feel relief.

Her hands hadn't stopped shaking since Ian had showed up in his Camaro, looking just as carefree, dangerous and sexy as he always had.

She'd wanted to feel nothing for him. Indifference would've been great. But, oh God, it hadn't been that easy. It had never been that easy.

One thing Ian had always been so good at was getting her to feel. Whether it was anger, whether it was desire, whether it was love…

Despite the mental roadblocks she put up against the memory of their first meeting, it still came back to play in her head…

❧

"BRADY VANDERCAMP JUST asked me out for tacos."

Sarah glanced up from fixing her ponytail and raised an eyebrow at her friend's announcement.

Still in her cheerleading uniform, her friend was grinning from ear to ear.

"Tacos? Seriously? Is that what we're calling it nowadays?"

"Oh stop. Yes, just Mexican food. It's at that place downtown." She twirled the end of a strand of red hair. "I think I'm going to go. He's so totally hot."

Brady might've been hot and the high school quarterback, but he was also a total manwhore.

"You want a condom to prevent that STD?" Sarah couldn't help but quip.

Kenzie wrinkled her nose. "As if I'd sleep with him. Just hoping for some make-out time. I hear he can kiss like—"

"Eew, no details please. It's cool, Kenzie. I'll call my dad and have him pick me up."

"Don't do that. Come with us. He said he'd ask Pete to

come if you wanted to go."

Pete? Double yuck. Brady's best friend was equally sleazy and couldn't seem to tell his head from his ass.

"I've got homework. I really need to go. Like I said, I can call my dad for a ride, or even walk home."

"But you don't have to. My brother was going to pick us up. He just got a new car and Dad says it's part of his responsibility."

Sarah hesitated as she zipped up her bag. "Which brother?"

"Ian."

"I'll walk."

"No, please don't. Look, I know he's got somewhat of a bad reputation—"

"Somewhat?"

"And I know he looks a little intimidating…"

"Hmmph."

"But he's nice. He's a good guy, Sarah. I promise. I wouldn't send you home with a psychopath." Kenzie grinned. "Those are strictly outlawed in my family anyway. Please, Sarah. And, umm, I just need a tiny favor. If you could just tell Ian that I'm staying after to study."

Sarah snorted. "Right. He'll buy that."

"He might."

"Fine. I'll catch a ride with your brother."

"Awesome. He'll be outside the front office at five, so you should head over. He's driving a beat-up Camaro."

"Sounds reassuring."

Not even five minutes later Sarah stood on the sidewalk with her backpack on one shoulder and her duffel bag on the other.

When a red Camaro squealed into the parking lot and raced toward the curb, she took a quick step back.

Heavy alternative music poured from the open windows as the car jerked to a stop.

Swallowing against a lump of unease, Sarah cast a glance back at the school and wondered if she should just reconsider and give her dad a call.

Then it was too late, because the driver's side door opened and Ian McLaughlin stepped out.

She knew very little about Kenzie's brother Ian. Only that he was a year older than them and a senior. He was notorious for getting into trouble, tended to skip classes more often than attend, and yet the girls seemed to love him.

Maybe it boiled down to that theory that some girls just loved a bad boy. Especially one as cute as Ian. His hair was a light brown and held shades of red depending on the light. He must've used some kind of gel to get his hair into that messy, tousled—and yet somehow totally sexy—style.

Rounding the car, Ian slid his sunglasses over his eyes and onto his head. Her gaze immediately landed on the deep groove of a several-inch-long scar near his eye.

"One cheerleader, when I was promised two."

Oh, he definitely had that faint lilt of a Scottish accent

going on. Her heart whumped in her chest and Sarah shifted her weight, wishing she'd thought to change out of her uniform.

"Your sister had to stay late and study." She cleared her throat. "I'm her friend, Sarah. I hope you don't mind if I catch a ride home still?"

"Study, you say? Hmm." He arched a brow and slowly approached. He was probably close to six feet and he towered over her barely five foot frame.

Flushed, and not even sure why, Sarah swallowed hard and simply nodded.

"Aye, I'll drive you home." He suddenly grinned, and it was so unexpected, so dazzling, her breath caught in her throat.

Was her heart pounding faster? Why? He couldn't hear it, could he? Jeez, this had been a bad idea.

Still, when he opened the passenger door, she slid in as delicately as her uniform allowed, to avoid exposing too much skin.

It was one thing about cheerleading she hadn't been thrilled about. The tacky, somewhat slutty uniforms. But Kenzie had talked her into trying out for the team—especially because she had so many strengths from being in gymnastics for years.

A moment later all time for second thoughts was gone as he slid behind the wheel and hit the gas.

Grabbing the *oh shit* handle, Sarah couldn't stop a small

gasp as her life flashed before her eyes.

"You really should slow down," she squeaked out.

"Life is too short to take it slow."

"Well, if you're dead does it matter?"

He laughed and shook his head. "Relax."

When he turned the car onto the highway, she frowned and shot him a quick glance.

"Hey, my parents' house is up by the navy base—you're heading south."

"Taking a different route. Scenic view."

Scenic view? Her dad had been stationed at NAS Whidbey for the past six years, and she wasn't sure what Ian meant by scenic view, but she gave him the benefit of the doubt.

Well, until he pulled up beneath a cluster of trees along a cliff that overlooked Puget Sound.

When he turned off the engine she cast him a furtive look. "What's going on? Is your car okay?"

"Car is great." He shifted in his seat and before she realized what he was doing, he reached out and cupped the side of her face. "Damn, you are a pretty thing."

Flustered and more than a little confused, she shook her head.

"Ian—"

He leaned forward and kissed her. Shock made her mind go white. The pressure of his mouth increased and she gasped, which allowed his tongue to slide past her lips. There was outrage inside her, but it was bullied aside by the surprising liquid heat seeping through her blood.

When he lifted his head, she realized she was clutching his shirt.

"Mmm. Very nice." His hand, which she didn't see move, suddenly came to rest on her leg. "These uniforms are just so damn hot. But I don't think you got enough thigh showing beneath that skirt."

The light touch of his fingers tracing up her thigh beneath her skirt—even while making her tingle and burn—snapped her into reality.

She slapped his hand away and scooted as far to her side of the car as she could.

"What are you *doing*?"

His grin, lazy and almost patronizing, widened. "Whatever you want me to do, doll."

"*Doll*? What, are you channeling Frank Sinatra? I want you to drive me home. I thought we had that covered."

"Sure you do." He inched forward, reaching for her again. "My sister doesn't study. I get it. It was a way to be alone with me. Creative, I admit."

Sarah sputtered, shaking her head. Dammit, she knew the studying line wouldn't work, but she hadn't seen this coming.

"I'm not trying to be alone with you. In fact I had every intention of walking my butt home until your sister insisted I should go with you."

His smile twitched and he looked suitably skeptical. "Seriously?"

"Seriously. You're not even my type." Or she hadn't thought he was, but something about that kiss…

His mouth tightened slightly now with derision. "Jocks are?"

"Not really, I like a guy who—wait, you know what? I don't need to explain my type to you. Take me home, please. Or I'll walk."

"Relax. Whatever you want, doll. I'll take you home." He paused. "You wanna share a joint before we go?"

She wrinkled her nose and folded her arms across her chest. "Did you *seriously* just offer me weed?"

"Try it. It'll relax you."

"Oh this just gets better and better. Look, I don't do marijuana and if ever did my dad would kill me."

"Ah. Got it. You're a daddy's girl, huh?"

Her head was going to explode into a million little bits because she was resisting the urge to hit him.

"Hey, here's an idea. *You* need to just stop talking."

He laughed and started the car. After she told him where to go, they spent the rest of the ride in silence.

When they pulled up in front of her house she scrambled to get out.

"Hey," he called out, before she could make her escape. "You've got a sweet, lush mouth, doll. I wouldn't mind exploring a little more if you change your mind. Let me know."

Not holding back in the least now, she gave him the finger and ran into her house, vowing to kill Kenzie the first chance she got.

✑

IF ONLY SHE'D had the sense to stick to her initial impression of him and stayed away.

Sarah blinked the memory from her mind and turned from the window to glance around the house.

She closed her eyes and drew in a slow breath. The air still held the faint scent of cumin and other spices.

Leaving India in her twenties hadn't diluted Gran's love for cooking dishes from her country. Kaali Daal, a black lentil dish, had always been Sarah's favorite.

She could almost taste the decadent food on her tongue. It was too easy to envision Gran chatting with her as she stood over the stove.

Tears pricked at her closed eyes and she opened them, drawing in an unsteady breath.

"I'm so sorry, Gran," she whispered to an empty room. "I should have come back sooner."

Of course there was no answer, but the air felt a little thicker and warmer, and she could almost feel her gran's presence reassuring her.

Regret made the tears Sarah had been fighting spill free. This time she made no attempt to stop them.

Chapter Three

"GIVE ME A Glenfiddich 18. Neat." Ian kept his hands folded and his gaze on the bar counter, but he could still feel the surprise in his eldest brother's stare.

The pub was near empty—apparently Old Man Cooper had gone home already as well.

"You do realize it's just about lunchtime." Aleck made his way down the bar until he was positioned right in front of him. "And you've gone and ordered one of the most expensive spirits we have?"

"You think I'm daft, big brother? Shut your mouth and just pour it already." Scowling, Ian lifted his head to make sure his brother hadn't taken offense.

Aleck, the eldest of all the McLaughlin kids was now sole owner of the pub. He didn't seem the slightest bit offended by his brother's comments. He was used to Ian's quick temper. Instead, his green eyes crinkled around the edges with laughter and his mouth was twisted into a slight smirk.

"Aye, I'll give ya your drink. So long as you fill me in on why the fook you're in such a foul mood." Aleck's accent had always been the thickest and slowest to fade.

"As if you don't know." Ian accepted the shot and glared at his brother. "Go bring Kenzie a tire, you say. As if you don't know just who exactly you were throwing in my path."

"No. I haven't a clue."

The genuine bewilderment on Aleck's face convinced him that maybe his brother wasn't lying.

"Look, Kenzie called and said she was in a bit of a mess and needed me to come out and bring her a tire. She didn't say she was with anyone." Aleck placed the bottle of scotch back up on the shelf with the other bottles of spirits. "Fill me in already. Who was with her?"

"Sarah," Ian finally growled.

"Sorry, who? Tera?"

Ian tipped back the scotch and slammed the glass on the bar. "*Sarah*."

"Sarah?" Aleck went still and tilted his head. "As in *your* Sarah? The good girl you shagged around with in your youth?"

"Aye. That'd be her." He stared into his empty shot glass, not seeing the drop of amber liquid, but instead the image of Sarah half-naked in the back of his Camaro. "And I wouldn't necessarily call her a good girl."

"Wasn't she now? One step from the nunnery from the impression I got." Aleck grinned. "Though I'm sure any corruption she experienced back then was your doing."

"Hmm. Maybe." The single malt scotch had warmed his

insides and taken the sharp edges off the memory of his encounter with Sarah.

"So, how was it seeing her again?"

"Oh just fucking fantastic." He gave a harsh laugh and pushed the empty glass to his brother. "Nearly as fantastic as taking a foot to the balls, I'd imagine."

"That lovely? Was she mean? Did she go and hurt your feelings?" Aleck teased good-naturedly.

"No." Ian hesitated, unable to share the humor. "More like I hurt her. I probably said some things I shouldn't have."

Aleck nodded. "Well, it wouldn't be the first time either one of you has let your temper best you. You want another drink?"

"No." Ian thrust a hand through his hair. "Wait, aye. One more."

His brother grabbed the bottle and poured another glass. "I'm sorry. But let me guess. She's fallen toward the ugly side and is as warm and cuddly as a porcupine?"

"Perhaps on the porcupine bit, but she's not ugly." He drank the second round. "She's prettier now, if you can believe it."

"Hmm. I'm trying to remember her. Short?"

"Petite. And she'd punch you in the stomach if she heard you call her short."

"Which is probably as high as she can reach," Aleck mused. "Long black hair, I think?"

Ian nodded.

"Aye, I remember her hair. She was a pretty thing. Quite exotic. She had that hint of olive skin, but blue eyes. I'm surprised you captured her interest. Back then she was too innocent for the likes of you."

And maybe still was. He'd calmed down considerably from what he'd been in his teen years. But he wasn't an idiot. Ian knew his reputation on the island, and his bad boy image hadn't fully gone away. Then again, he hadn't done much to dissuade it.

"Will you see her again?"

"I doubt it. I don't think she cared much for seeing me today, to be honest."

"Aye, well you didn't end on the best terms. Am I right?"

No. They certainly hadn't. Just the memory of it was like taking a two-by-four to the chest. His jaw clenched against the wave of guilt and pain. Both emotions had been violently at war that day—as much as they still were now. Beneath those two emotions had been another one. Bitter disappointment. And it was always there. Hot and dark, running a river of anger through his blood.

He didn't think about it much. Couldn't go there in his head, because it was all such a mind fuck.

"There's a reason the past is behind you." Aleck's quiet words resonated through the warm haze the Glenfiddich had left.

"Aye. And it'll stay there—no need to worry about that."

"Good. No need to be digging up old dirt. Besides,

you've got Gina now. I'd almost wager you're serious about her."

Ian's lips quirked. Almost serious meaning he'd been casually dating her for two months. Or really, they'd mostly just hooked up. Though in his world, that was nearly a lifetime.

The only exception had been Sarah. They'd been together for almost seven months. His half-smile faltered and he shook his head. That didn't mean much—only that he'd been young and stupid.

"Damn, Ian. Who shit on your parade?"

The soft feminine question had him glancing up and giving a slow grin to Delonna, the bartender scheduled to work the swing shift.

"A fourteen-thousand-pound elephant, if you'd believe it," he murmured and gave her a glance-over. "Hello, Delonna."

Her wavy blonde hair was drawn up in a ponytail and her blue-green eyes were narrowed on him with open curiosity.

She was young, maybe twenty-three, and an absolute stunner. She always brought in a good amount of tips on the nights she worked. While he hadn't worked at the pub in years, Ian made himself available now and then on a busy day and he'd seen how popular she was.

He'd asked her out. Once. And she'd turned him down gently, using the "better off friends" line. It had been hard not to take offense at the time, even if nowadays she was just like another little sister to him.

"Seriously. You look all brooding and scary. Like, more than normal. Are you and Gina fighting?"

Gina. No, they hadn't been fighting. Hell, they hadn't even spoken in days.

"No, we're doing grand." Though grand might've been pushing it.

"He ran into an ex-girlfriend," Aleck called out from the other end of the counter.

Delonna glanced down his older brother's way. "Really now? That can have the potential to wreck anyone's day."

"It didn't wreck my day, dammit. It just threw me. I haven't seen her in years." And then when he did, first chance he'd got, he'd made her feel like shit.

"Weird. Usually you're the one agitating the ladies, but it seems like it's swinging the other way this time." Delonna cleared her throat when Aleck shot her a sharp look. "I could be wrong though."

"A little discretion, Delonna?" Aleck muttered as his scowl darkened.

She had the decency to flush. "Right. Let me just look that word up again. Always good to see you, Ian." She shook her head and moved out from behind the bar, making her way to the kitchen.

"Sorry, sometimes her filter is a bit rusty," Aleck apologized as he stared after the blonde bartender.

"It's Delonna. Not much of a surprise there. We forgive her because she's got a lovely arse."

"Watch your mouth," Aleck grumbled, glancing away from the retreating blonde. "You shouldn't be checking out her arse."

"I'm not. Actually haven't in years. She's all yours."

His brother grunted and shook his head. "She's practically a child. Far too young for my liking. Besides, the last thing I need is a woman right now."

"Bollocks. You should be getting laid, and often."

Aleck threw his head back and laughed—a low, rumbling sound that resonated in the bar.

"I never said I wasn't enjoying female companionship, little brother."

Ian grinned and shook his head. "Aye. You're a true McLaughlin. You taught me everything I know."

"Not everything." Aleck's amusement seemed to fade some and his eyes clouded. "You should go see Gina. It'll take your mind off of…things."

"Maybe I should." Ian slid the shot glasses back toward his brother and stood up. "Thanks for the drink. What do I owe you?"

"Bartend for me the Friday night of Labor Day weekend. We'll need the extra help."

"Done."

Aleck collected the glasses and set them in the sink behind the bar. "Can you drive?"

"Aye. What do you take me for, a novice? It'd take three times that amount to begin to addle my mind."

"Of course. Whatever was I thinking?" Aleck came around the bar and hugged him. "Love ya, wee Ian."

Though Ian wasn't short by any means, Aleck certainly could get away with the wee comment. While Ian had inherited more of his mother's looks, Aleck had taken after Da. Still the McLaughlin green eyes, but with darker hair and an impressive height that ensured he towered over most men.

Aleck gave him a thump on his back and then pulled away. "Go have fun. You'll forget all about the other one."

The one that got away. The thought raced through his head before he could stop it. And it lingered as he made the drive to his shop in Coupeville instead.

It was a good thing she'd left him, he told himself. With Gina, what you saw was what you got. She swore like a sailor, was aggressive sexually, had a body like a pin-up girl, and had a streak of meanness that could come out with enough provocation or alcohol. But together, the two of them worked. It complemented the dark side of him so many wanted to deny was real.

Sarah seemed so sweet and innocent. Lovely and delicate in a way that made men pause and stare. But if you didn't look beyond the front, you might get blindsided. She could turn on you in an instant. Once she had your heart, she could destroy it with the precision and calculation of a military missile.

Yes. If he were smart, he'd avoid her until she'd once again left the island.

～

SARAH GLANCED IN the mirror and adjusted the delicate purple scarf she'd added to her khaki skirt and black crossover top.

The scarf had been Gran's and she'd added it to her outfit at the last minute. She was due at the lawyer's office in fifteen minutes and if she didn't start walking, she'd be late.

She'd already slept in longer than planned this morning. After a long phone call with Emily, she'd spent her evening struggling with painful memories. Not to mention the attempt to spend time on her latest project. She was fortunate enough to be able to travel with her work. Being a freelance graphic designer didn't always bring in a ton of money, but fortunately the online projects allowed her to work from anywhere.

Sarah lingered for just a moment more, bringing the scarf to her nose and closing her eyes as she inhaled.

There was still the hint of her gran's perfume, and tears pricked behind Sarah's closed lids.

With an unsteady, but determined breath in, she opened her eyes and grabbed her purse.

A few minutes later she was walking down the street toward the small law office in downtown Coupeville. The town had expanded some since she'd been here last. More people had moved into the charming area, but it was still quite small, with most things within comfortable walking distance. A place where everybody seemed to know everybody, and she could feel the probing gazes as she walked down the street.

Maybe she looked familiar and they were trying to place exactly who she was. Or maybe they knew. But if she wasn't already, she knew it wouldn't be too long before she was the talk of the town.

She found her stride increasing until, with some relief, she entered the small building that housed Gran's lawyer's office.

He was a small man, probably close to seventy, but his gaze was sharp and his grip was strong when he grasped her hand.

"Ms. Rawlings. I've heard quite a bit about you. I'm William Yates." He smiled and gestured to a chair.

"Nice to finally meet you in person, Mr. Yates." Once she had sat with her hands folded in her lap, she met his gaze.

"You look like your grandmother." For a moment the all-business expression slipped from his face, replaced instead by something softer. Sadder.

How well had he known Gran? Sarah knew he'd been her lawyer for at least the last decade, but had their relationship gone beyond the professional? She wasn't about to ask.

"Do I?" She gave a small shrug. "I've always been told I take after my father's side more."

"Perhaps the eyes, yes. But in other ways…you resemble her so much." He cleared his throat and reached for a folder on his desk. "Here is a copy of Libby's will. As I explained during our phone call, she does have a condition that you live in the house for the duration of one calendar month before you are able to place it on the market, should you decide to sell. If you can't meet this condition, the house will be given to your younger sister with the same understanding."

Sarah stared at the words, her throat tightening as the lawyer clarified them aloud. Her sister had a rich husband, and rarely saw anyone because they were off traveling the world. They didn't need another house. Sarah on the other hand…

But a month on the island? She'd known about the condition, and yet hearing it aloud, the finality of it, made the blood rush from her head. She clutched the leather handles of the chair, steadying herself as she grew a bit dizzy.

It wouldn't have been a problem if it weren't for one person. One person with deep green eyes that left her heart pounding and her head a complete mess.

"Do you think you'll be able to meet this condition, Ms. Rawlings?"

"What?" She blinked, focusing again on the printed will in front of her. It was all legal speak and seemed as foreign to her as if it had been written in German. "I, umm, yes. I've made plans to spend the month of July out here."

It was June 29th. She was only a couple of days early from starting the countdown of the month of hell. Not that she didn't love Whidbey—who wouldn't love the island? It was Ian. It had always been Ian…

"Did your daughter join you on the island for the summer?"

"No. Emily is spending the month with her grandmother in Florida." She glanced back up and gave a forced smile. "Bonding time. You understand, I'm sure."

"I see."

Was that disappointment in the older man's eyes? If so, it was hard to decipher as he quickly slipped his reading glasses back on.

He continued touching on several points in the will that she needed to be aware of, but most of it she'd already grasped.

By the time she left the office, copy of the will in hand, she was emotionally exhausted and ready for a nap. Or a glass of wine.

Wine would have to wait until she made a trip to the store. Which was actually the next thing on her to-do list. The fridge was empty.

She'd fallen asleep without dinner last night, and hadn't even realized she hadn't eaten until she'd woken up with a growling stomach.

Grabbing her phone, she dialed her mother's house. Emily answered on the second ring.

"Hi, Mom! Grandma said it was probably you." Her daughter's chipper voice coiled around Sarah's heart, and her throat tightened as tears pricked at her eyes.

She missed Emily so much. This would be the longest they'd ever been apart.

"Hi, sweetie. Are you behaving for your grandma?"

"Yeah. But she watches a lot of stupid shows on TV, and she tells me the Disney channel will rot my brain."

The unhappiness in her daughter's voice had Sarah smiling reluctantly.

"A break from TV isn't a bad thing. You should go outside more and practice your gymnastics."

"It's too hot outside. I feel gross if I'm out there for more than a few minutes. I hate Grandma's house."

Emily had never liked hot weather. For just a second, the thought of what it would be like to move them both to the island flitted through her mind. Emily would love the mild weather in the Pacific Northwest. But it was impossible. She'd spend the required month here and then she'd sell the house. There was no other choice.

"I know it's a little hot. Maybe you guys can catch a movie."

"I dunno. I miss you, Mom."

"I miss you too, sweetie. So much." Tears did fill her eyes now, and she resented the fact that she was being forced to stay here for a month. "Hey, tell me how Bubba is handling the stay at Grandma's?"

Once her daughter launched into an excited conversation about her chubby Chihuahua, Sarah knew her daughter was sufficiently distracted from her unhappiness at being banished to Grandma's house for the summer.

When Sarah hung up the phone a few minutes later, though, she knew her own unhappiness wasn't so easily dismissed.

Her phone buzzed again and she frowned, wondering who would be texting. Her mother didn't even own a cell phone and would've just called her back.

Sarah stared at the message and smiled slightly.

Kenzie who was at work. She wanted her to drop by the pub and hang out, fill her in on how the lawyer's visit had gone.

No way. Not going to happen. Sarah started to put her phone away, deciding to text her back later, when a second text popped up.

And I promise the brother with jerk tendencies won't be there. He's at work.

Unable to stop a soft laugh, Sarah shook her head. Most of her hesitation at going to see Kenzie had been because of Ian. But if he really wasn't going to be there...

It would be good to go see her friend. Kenzie would be a good distraction from how much Sarah was missing her daughter. And then she could have that glass of wine…

Before she could overthink it, she hit reply and told Kenzie she'd be there within a half hour.

WHY SARAH TOOK the time to reapply her lip gloss and fluff her hair was beyond her comprehension.

She wasn't trying to look good for anyone. Not that the person she was most concerned about would even be there.

McLaughlin's Pub was off a side street in Oak Harbor. It literally looked like someone's small one-story home that had been gutted and made into a bar.

When she stepped inside, though, there was no denying the place was a Scottish pub. The national flag of Scotland was placed throughout the connecting rooms of the pub in no less than four spots, along with photos—some autographed—of various celebrities native to Scotland.

The place was dim, the stage in the back currently empty. But there was music piped in from hidden speakers, and her throat tightened as she recognized the band Simple Minds. The song playing, "Don't You Forget About Me", seemed a little too apt.

Surprisingly, it was fairly busy for a Tuesday afternoon. It was weird being here now, knowing she was of legal age to stay until closing time, instead of being kicked out by eight because she was a minor.

So many changes. So much time had passed.

"So the rumors are true."

Following the sound of the voice, Sarah's gaze darted to the extended bar counter to her right. Tall and dark, with an expression that held only warm curiosity, Aleck McLaughlin watched her from where he stood framed by the various beers on tap.

Her stomach clenched as she summoned a polite smile. Well. Apparently the rule still held that all McLaughlins must be attractive.

"Hello, Aleck. It's been a while."

"Aye." He gestured to an empty barstool. "Have a seat. Kenzie is in the kitchen at the moment, but she'll be out shortly. I assume you came to see her?"

"You'd assume right." She pulled out the barstool and sat, folding her hands in her lap. "Could I get a glass of merlot? I'm not picky."

He winked and reached for a bottle behind the bar. "Well lucky for you I am picky. I'll only give you the best."

"I appreciate it." She accepted the glass a moment later and took a small sip. He hadn't been kidding—it was definitely one of the better wines she'd tasted.

"You made it!" Kenzie slid onto the empty barstool next to her a moment later. "I want to hear everything the lawyer said."

Sarah grimaced. "Everything? I'm not sure even I re-member everything."

"Well the big points. And I see you've got wine already—must've been a doozy." She glanced at her brother. "Aleck, give me a pint of the African Amber Ale."

Aleck folded his arms across a broad chest and arched a brow. "You do realize you're working, Kenzie?"

"I'm on my break." She rolled her eyes. "Now don't be an arse, and pour me my beer already."

Surely there were regulations about that kind of thing, Sarah thought, but smothered a laugh when Aleck dutifully went to pour the beer.

Kenzie had always had her brothers twisted around her finger. It seemed some things never changed.

"Now." Kenzie turned back and propped her elbows on the smooth bar surface. "Tell me about this morning."

Chapter Four

IAN WIPED A dirty hand down the front of his coveralls and stepped back from the '65 Corvette, giving it a narrowed glance.

"How's it coming along, boss?" Frank, one of his employees, stopped by to check out the 'Vette.

"Just replaced the front panel." Ian patted the hood. "Another couple days and I think this bad boy will be ready to go."

"It's looking awesome. We just got in a '41 Willys Pickup, pretty sweet condition. They're asking for some rust removal and a paint job."

"Easy enough. I'll check it out in a minute."

"You should. But, hey, wanted to let you know that your phone has been going off."

"Thanks. I'll check it out." Ian dropped a stained rag onto the counter and headed toward the small office at the back of the shop.

He picked up his phone and saw several missed texts from Aleck. He clicked on the first one.

Stay away from the pub for the next couple hours. She's here.

Ian frowned. She? Sarah? He read the next text.

And that would be Sarah in case you're a bit daft.

His lips quirked and he read the final message.

Apparently she's staying for at least a month. It's a condition of the will if she's to inherit the house. And I swear I must've grown a vagina with all my gossiping.

Ian did laugh now, and typed in a quick reply that he'd avoid the pub. Because the last thing he wanted was to run in to Sarah again. He was still irritated from the first encounter. And held a bit of guilt, if he let himself admit it.

The next half hour he kept himself immersed in his work, but as lunchtime rolled around and he had nothing to eat, the idea of dropping by the pub had more appeal.

There was always a free meal available and it wasn't unusual to drop by on his lunch break to go visit Kenzie and Aleck if they were working. Why shouldn't he go?

Because Sarah's there today, his conscience reminded him. *You don't want to aggravate her.*

Ah, but he did. The devil on his shoulder was itching to stir up shit. To watch the anger and shock on her face if he were to show up for lunch.

Then there was the sentimental side of him, which barely existed anymore, that wanted any reason to be near her again. Because it was Sarah. The only woman who'd ever slipped so deeply into his soul.

He sent a quick text to Gina and then grabbed his keys.

"Going to lunch. Back in an hour," he called out before he left the shop.

Driving from the small shop in Coupeville to Oak Harbor was only about a ten or fifteen minute drive, but it was plenty of time to let his mind wander.

∽

"YOU KNOW YOU'RE lucky you don't break your back doing that."

Ian nearly laughed at the look of incredulity on Sarah's face as she turned to face him.

With her hands on her hips, she was breathing hard from the series of handsprings she'd just done on the grass field. The black leggings and dark tank top hugged her body perfectly and showed off her petite, toned, athlete's body.

"Seriously? You again?"

"I'm picking up Kenzie," he drawled and crossed the grass toward her. "Do you need a ride?"

A look of discomfort flickered across her face and she looked away. "Kenzie is staying late. She didn't call you?"

"No. And I assume by staying late you mean hanging out with Brady Vandercamp again?"

Surprise showed on Sarah's face, but she didn't reply.

"It's cool. My sister is overdue for a little fun." He

stopped in front of Sarah. "You too, I'd bet."

Her chin came up and she tossed her head, sending her long black ponytail flying. "Whatever fun I may or may not be having is none of your concern, Ian McLaughlin."

"We could make it mine. You're really good at that handspring stuff for being just a cheerleader."

"I'm not just a cheerleader. I'm on the gymnastics team too."

"Nice." He grinned. "I bet you look hot in one of those spandex bathing suit type things."

"Oh, you are such a jerk." Her words were terse, but her cheeks filled with a pretty blush and he saw the flicker of pleasure in her eyes before she looked away.

Amusement eased through him and his smile widened. When he took another step toward her, so that they were just inches apart, she stepped back.

"Why do you keep running from me?"

"Because I'm a smart girl who knows she should avoid the bad boys."

Before he could blink she'd turned and sprinted away from him. Her pace increased until she threw herself into another series of handsprings.

Only this time, on the last one, something happened when she landed. With a sharp cry of pain, she fell to the ground and clutched her ankle.

Not by any means an athlete, Ian surprised himself by how quickly he reached her side.

He fell to his knees and probed her ankle with gentle hands. "You land on your foot wrong? Does this hurt?"

"Ouch! Yes." Tears filled her eyes and she bit her lip. "I think I heard a snap. Oh no, what if it's broken? I'm so screwed. This is all your fault."

"My fault?" He scowled and lifted her into his arms.

"Yes, dammit you distracted me." She wound her arms around his neck, clinging to him. "And you're doing it again."

He glanced down, gauging her face for the amount of pain she was in. Pretty bad, going by her pinched expression and the glaze of agony in her eyes.

His concern spiked and he increased his stride to his car. "How am I distracting you?"

"Not—oh God it hurts—telling. Where are you taking me?"

"To the hospital. Do I need to take you to the one on base?"

"Either one. My dad's insurance lets me go anywhere. Look, you don't have to take me—"

"I'm not leaving you. Hang on a sec." He set her down gently, keeping one arm around her waist. "No pressure on the hurt foot, okay?"

He dug his keys out of his pocket and opened the car door. After knocking the pack of cigarettes off the passenger seat, he eased her in and then buckled her up.

Several hours later, when she'd been x-rayed and diagnosed at the ER, he again helped her outside to the car. This time she was on crutches and touting a hairline fracture.

Sarah's navy dad was apparently out at sea on a ship, but her mom had come by the hospital initially with the insurance information and to check on her daughter. But despite the mom's worries, Sarah's antsy little sister had made it difficult for the two to stay.

After the assurance that Sarah would be fine and a promise that Ian would drive her home safely, the mom and younger sister had left.

"Thank you." Sarah rolled her head to look at him, a wide, relaxed grin on her face. "My mom pretty much thinks you're the best thing since sliced bread."

"Really now? How are those painkillers working out for you?"

"The drugs are wonderful." Sarah drew out the "uh" in wonderful. "And my mom?" She waggled a finger at him. "You've charmed her, but little does she know it's all an illusion."

He laughed and caught her finger, pressing a kiss to the fleshy underside. "An illusion you say? I think I'm quite a bit better than sliced bread, actually."

He didn't miss the way her breath hitched and her lips parted. "Yeah. You kind of are. Do you miss Scotland?"

Shite, she wanted to talk about Scotland? He'd much preferred the other conversation.

"Sometimes. But after four years I'm pretty settled here.

Besides, there's a lot I like about the States too."

She waggled her brows. "American girls?"

"Aye," he said softly. "At this moment, most definitely an American girl."

Her eyes widened to crystalline pools of blue. Had he shocked her? Embarrassed her?

She opened her mouth, and he suspected she would blister him with a reply.

"You are ridiculously hot, Ian McLaughlin."

All right, that was *not* what he'd expected. And he definitely wasn't about to protest.

A lazy smile curved his mouth. "You think I'm hot?"

"Oh yeah." She nodded and leaned toward him. "And you know it too."

Ah, the truth came out under the influence of drugs. Pure masculine satisfaction slid through him. "I lied. Kenzie did call to cancel her ride today. I was just hoping you'd let me drive you home."

Her mouth parted. "You did?"

"Oh yeah."

"I'm glad."

He cupped the back of her neck and tilted his head down.

"You know what else?" she murmured. "You're nicer than you want people to believe."

He frowned, her words not sitting well with him. "I'm not nice."

And he proved it by kissing her. Slowly and deeply.

But it didn't matter. He needed to taste her again. Touch her. And if it had to be a stolen kiss while she was drugged to the hilt, then whatever.

IAN BLINKED AWAY the memory as he turned the corner that eased into Oak Harbor.

Only as the days had gone by and she'd eased off the pain meds, Sarah hadn't seemed to regret the kiss or make any attempt to distance herself from him.

He'd followed her around school, carrying her books while she'd hobbled on crutches. He was late to almost every class—not that that was anything new. Just the reasons for it had changed.

For once the temptation to actually go to class—and chance passing her in the hall—had been stronger than skipping.

They'd been together non-stop, and when they couldn't be together physically, they were sneaking in phone calls and expensive texts.

And the crazy thing was, she wouldn't sleep with him— and he'd never been the type of guy who waited around for sex when plenty of girls were willing.

But he did wait for her. And as clichéd as it was, the night they finally made love was after his prom that she'd talked him into attending. She'd been a virgin and there'd been something heady and primitive about being her first. He'd wanted to be her last. Couldn't imagine his life with any other girl.

And once the sexual seal was broken after that night, they couldn't keep their hands off each other. Were together as much as they could be.

Looking back on it now, he knew without a doubt it wouldn't have been long before he started thinking about ring shopping. At eighteen. Christ, he'd been stupid.

Because one night had proven it all a lie. Everything he'd believed about her—about himself—was proven wrong.

One night was all it took to slice Sarah neatly from his life.

He pulled his Camaro up outside the pub a few minutes later and stared at the propped-open door and the darkness inside.

Maybe he was stupid for coming here today—actually, there was no denying he was. If he had any sense, he'd throw the car in reverse and get the hell back to Coupeville. Stay away from Sarah and all the trouble she was.

But he'd never had much sense, so why the hell start now?

Spotting the car that pulled up beside him, he gave a wave and climbed out of the Camaro.

∽

SARAH SET HER glass of wine back on the bar to avoid

spilling it as she snorted back a laugh.

"You are so funny, Kenzie." She shook her head and grimaced. "Some things never change."

Her friend gave an innocent shrug, her eyes wide. "What? I'm not trying to be funny. I'm just telling you about my last date. Seriously. How would you have reacted if you showed up to dinner and the guy asked to be addressed as Mr. Pleasure Hands?"

"Umm, I'd have walked out."

"And I'd rather not hear any of this, thank you very much," Aleck drawled from behind the counter and shook his head. "And, Kenzie, I believe your break is over now. Or rather, a half hour ago?"

"Such a hard-arse." She rolled her eyes and hopped down from the barstool. But when she rounded the bar she pressed a smacking kiss on her brother's cheek. "Thanks for the extended lunch, Aleck."

"You're welcome, kid."

Sarah bit back a sigh at how sweet the siblings were together. Aleck had always been nice, though. Colin too, even if she didn't know him all that well—only that he was the more well-behaved twin. While Ian loved to get in trouble, Colin was likely off doing some good deed.

Both had been equally charming with the girls, though.

"Ah shite."

The muttered curse had Sarah glancing up at Aleck. His mouth was compressed into a line of displeasure, and his wary gaze was on the doorway.

Crap. Her heart sank and she knew who'd just entered the pub without turning around.

"You can't be serious," Kenzie joined in with a growl.

Yup. Sarah snuck a quick glance to the door, and even though the sunshine behind him turned him into a silhouette, she'd be able to pick his form out of a lineup any day.

Only Ian wasn't alone. A busty blonde in tiny shorts and a skintight tank, proclaiming her *Satan's Bitch*, clung to his arm.

Ouch. It shouldn't have hurt. It'd been eleven years since she'd considered Ian hers. That was over a decade to dump the immediate emotional response at seeing him.

And yet, not really. Seeing Ian's latest lover clinging to him hurt just as much as if Sarah and he had broken up the day before.

But she was damn careful so that he wouldn't see any pain in her eyes.

"Serious about what, little sis?" Ian moved slowly into the bar, his stride almost a swagger and his smile a taunt. "Just came for a bit of a lunch, if you don't mind."

"Oh, I mind quite a bit." Kenzie rounded the corner and glared, jamming a finger into Ian's chest. "Did Aleck text you?"

Sarah looked up at Aleck and caught the quick flash of guilt on the eldest McLaughlin brother's face.

"As I said, we're just here for lunch," Ian protested with a tone of innocence that nobody was buying.

"Hmmph. Fine. Go sit in the corner and I'll bring you out something in a minute." Kenzie shook her head.

Unable to look away, Sarah swallowed hard as he suddenly turned his gaze to hers. The amused light in them and mocking tilt to his mouth made her insides flutter. For a moment she thought he would ignore his sister and come right up to the bar and take the two empty barstools next to her. And when his gaze fell on the open seats she bit her lip to avoid a groan of disbelief.

But then he winked and gave a small shrug before turning and leading his chick of the hour to the corner table in the shadows.

"I'm so sorry about this, Sarah. I don't know what's gotten into him," Kenzie said softly, as she approached the bar again. Her gaze darted to her brother. "And you, Aleck, good job. You've officially joined Ian's name on my shit list. I can't believe you'd tell him she was here. I promised Sarah he wasn't around."

"We're all adults now, Kenzie." Aleck's brows were drawn together, and though there was regret in his eyes, his voice was terse. "It's a big island, but a small community. They're bound to run into each other."

"It's fine," Sarah agreed, her voice husky. "I'm nearly done with my lunch anyway. I should probably just leave."

Kenzie sighed. "Oh, please don't. We've only just had a few minutes together."

"We've had almost an hour." Keeping her tone gentle, Sarah pulled a twenty from her wallet and placed it on the counter. "This should cover my lunch."

Aleck pushed it back toward her. "It's on me. It's the least I can do. I'm sorry, Sarah."

Shaking her head, she refused to pick up the money. It didn't matter that it was almost the last of her cash and her checking account was running dry.

She hated feeling indebted to anyone, and owing any favors to a McLaughlin brother was just a bad idea in her book.

"I insist on paying." Sarah slid off the stool, which was high for her petite frame, and adjusted her purse. "Kenzie, give me a call and we can hang out at Gran's home one of these nights. Watch movies, eat Top Ramen. You know, just like the old days."

"Okay, I'll call you later." The apology was blatant in Kenzie's gaze as Sarah rushed past her to the door.

Outside in the sun, Sarah struggled for her eyes to adjust as she dug in her purse for the keys to Gran's car.

"Always on the run, I see."

Her fingers wrapped around the keys just as the soft, lilting voice reached her ears.

Dammit, he'd followed her outside? Heart thumping and mouth dry, she waited for Kenzie or Aleck's voice to demand he come back inside. But there was nothing, just silence.

As the seconds ticked by, her disbelief grew. She had to

face him. Alone. Sarah turned around, struggling desperately not to let every emotion rushing through her reflect on her face.

"What do you want?" She'd meant to say something clever. Flippant. Not only had she *not* managed that, but her question was almost a plea, infused with a faint anguish that was chronic when she thought of him.

His lopsided smile fell back into a grim slash and his gaze darkened. "Now there's a loaded question, aye?"

"Not really, no." She clenched her hands around her keys and turned away to unlock the door. "It should be fairly simple."

His hand fell past her to the door, holding it closed. "Well it's not. We should talk."

A laugh of disbelief ripped from her, but then it died and her throat went tight. "You want to talk? About what?"

"Fuck. I'm not even sure anymore."

Really that shouldn't shock her. He was making trouble, just because it's what he did best. "I'm only here for a month. Can we just make it a point to avoid each other?"

"How very adult of us," he mocked.

She spun around to face him, not bothering to hold back the frustration. "Maybe it isn't, but I think we said everything that needed to be said eleven years ago…" She trailed off as his expression slid from mocking to dark. Bitter.

"Aye," he said with deceptive softness. "Eleven years ago you were quite thorough in telling me how you really felt."

She could feel her cheeks flushing at the memory of that day—at the alternate personality she'd seemed to instantly develop. She smothered the quick rise of regret and guilt—because her words had been well deserved. Hadn't they?

"Which means there's not a lot left to say, right?" She pushed his arm away from her car door and succeeded in opening it this time. "Go back inside, Ian. I'm sure your bimbo girlfriend is getting lonely."

"Ouch." He gave a harsh laugh, but didn't stop her. "You're really quite good with the barbed insults for someone who tries hard to be known as the nice girl."

A response was on her tongue, but she refused to let it fly. Instead she climbed into her car, shut the door and drove off a moment later.

In the rearview she watched him move back into the pub, and she bit her lip.

He wanted to turn this on her? Make her look like the evil bitch? It wasn't fair. But then it'd never been fair.

"He's an asshole," she whispered. "He'll always be an asshole."

When tears filled her eyes, she gave a growl of dismay. She wouldn't cry over him. Not again.

She turned the old Chevy onto the main road and hit the gas. Impatiently, she wiped the moisture from her eyes and then cranked the radio to distract her.

One month. She just had to get through one month. And she'd do it by holing herself up at Gran's with some good books and her work to keep her busy.

She left Oak Harbor, roaring down the two-lane highway that was soon thickly lined by trees.

It was the tears in her eyes that delayed her spotting them. But when she finally focused on the deer and a small fawn moseying across the road ahead, Sarah slammed on her brakes.

She wouldn't be able to stop in time! A scream tore from her throat. Instinct, and the desire not to murder Bambi, had her swinging the wheel to the right.

The car veered off the road and even though she still had her foot on the brakes, she knew she was going to hit the tree.

Chapter Five

ON IMPACT EVERYTHING went red, before darkness rolled in momentarily. When she blinked back to alertness, pain had washed through her as she struggled to push aside the deflated airbag.

"Whoa." She patted herself down, checking to make sure nothing was bleeding or broken. Her head hurt like crazy and her muscles were overtly taut, but nothing seemed seriously wrong.

Her door was jerked open and the unfamiliar face of an elderly man stared down at her with concern, asking her something.

"What?" she shook her head, completely disoriented.

And then the man stepped back and another figure appeared, crouching down to talk to her.

"Ma'am, are you okay? Can you get out of the vehicle?"

Her heart rose in her throat and her eyes widened. For a moment she'd thought she was staring at Ian, but then the sheriff's uniform registered and she realized this wasn't her ex, but his equally attractive twin. The missing scar near his left eye was another clue it wasn't Ian.

"Colin?" Her voice croaked and she tried to make her way out of the car.

Colin's brows drew together in confusion, even as he rushed to help her climb out.

"Do I know you?" He paused and his lips pursed. "Aye, wait a minute. Sarah?"

She nodded, frustrated to feel her eyes filling with tears. It had already been too much. And now this? Crashing her car and being forced to face another McLaughlin family member?

"Are you hurt, luv?"

Shaking her head, she couldn't stop the tears from spilling down her cheeks. "No. No, I don't think so. A little sore, but okay I think."

"There you go, then. Take a deep breath." He caught her shoulders in his hands and gave them a gentle squeeze. "It's going to be all right. I promise."

What the hell was wrong with her? She was falling apart all over Ian's twin. But she suspected she would've had the same reaction to whoever had pulled her from the car.

The adrenaline pulsing through her body started to diminish and she scrubbed at her moist eyes.

She turned to look at her gran's car and let out a cry of dismay. The front was smashed in; the hood bent into an inverted V. And both airbags had deployed.

"Oh no," she whispered, shoving her hands through her

hair. "This looks bad."

"Aye. It doesn't look good. Can I call someone for you, Sarah?"

Kenzie was working. She shook her head, wishing she could just spout off the number of someone. Anyone. "No."

No one who was in Washington State anyway. Not since Gran had passed.

Colin asked another question, but she couldn't focus. She was too busy wondering how she was going to fix Gran's car—which was her only vehicle on the island. How could she afford it?

When Colin stepped away from her a moment later, it barely registered.

How had the island that had once been such a haven to her become such a constant state of hell?

～

"WHY ARE YOU so interested in her?"

Ian blinked, tearing his gaze away from the pool table where Gina was lining up another shot.

"Who?"

"That girl you just chased out of here." She rolled her eyes and took the shot. Missed by a mile.

"She's an old friend."

"One you used to fuck?" Her mouth curved into what she probably thought was a seductive little pout.

It did nothing for him. Not today. "That's none of your

damn business."

"You are such an asshole." Gina wove her arms around his neck and pressed her voluptuous body against his. "Mmm. And if you weren't so good in bed I'd be on to another guy by now."

She'd been exactly what he'd wanted a few months ago. All tits and arse, fun in bed and with no commitment. But lately she'd been turning him off like a cheap perfume.

"Hey, if that's what you want." He threw it out there, knowing she wouldn't bite, but almost hoping she would.

"I want you, babe. Though I'm kind of pissed we haven't done it in almost a month." She kissed him slow and deep, and lifted her head a minute later. "Come over after work tonight?"

Maybe a night with Gina would be good for clearing his mind—among other things. Sarah had twisted him up into a fucking emotional pretzel. She'd always had the ability to do that to him, and it had driven him nuts.

He needed to focus on someone else. Gina was probably the answer.

"I'll see what I can do." He stepped back, feeling his cell in his pocket start to buzz.

He dug out his phone as Kenzie walked by them, giving him a dirty look. Obviously she wasn't a fan of Gina's PDAs. He grinned at his sister and gave an overtly innocent shrug.

Seeing Colin's number on his caller ID, Ian answered, "This must be important if you're calling me from work."

"It's important."

Where Ian's tone had been a lazy drawl, his brother's was curt and grim. Pretty damn uncommon for his twin, actually.

"What's going on?" Ian moved away from Gina, lowering his voice.

"You're aware that Sarah's back on the isl—"

"Yes, I'm quite aware." His words flattened. "Is that why you've called?"

"No. She's been in an accident."

Everything inside Ian turned to ice, and his chest went impossibly tight to where he could barely speak.

"She's all right," Colin continued. "Just a bit banged up. I'm going to try and talk her into going to the hospital just to get checked out. But I called because—"

"Where is she?" Ian was already walking toward the door.

"About four miles outside of Oak Harbor on Highway 20."

"I'll be there in five minutes." He turned off the phone and dug into his pocket for his keys.

"Babe. What the hell?" Gina ran outside the pub after him, her mouth twisted in dismay. "You're leaving me?"

"I have to go check on someone. Sorry, G." He gave her a quick kiss, even though he still wasn't feeling it.

"Someone?" She folded her arms across her large chest and cocked a brow. "As in this old friend again? Seriously?"

Shit, he should've realized Gina would've picked up on

his interest in Sarah.

"I'll call you later," he promised. "You know I want to see you."

That last line might've been stretching it. If he admitted it, he'd only brought Gina here for lunch because he'd known it would needle Sarah.

"You'd better call me." She shook her head. "Because I got options, Ian. And you know it."

Jesus, she was becoming much more work than play.

Not bothering to reply, he jumped into his car and left the pub.

Almost five minutes later, as promised, he pulled up to the accident scene. The Island County Sheriff's cruiser was parked with lights flashing just behind Sarah's vehicle. It had veered off the road and was pretty much making out with a tree.

Ian's concern mounted as he climbed from his Camaro.

Right away he spotted Sarah. She and Colin stood next to her car, deep in discussion.

Her face was blotchy from tears and likely the airbag slamming into it. Ian's muscles tautened, and something dark and volatile built inside him as he watched his twin place an arm around her shoulders. Surely it was a gesture of comfort, but Ian didn't like it. And the realization both startled and irritated him.

She stilled, as if sensing him, and her body twisted his way, her gaze locking on him. For a moment he could've sworn there was relief in her eyes, before it slipped away into something close to disbelief and misery.

When he reached her side, Colin pulled away from Sarah. Her gaze was only on Ian, though, as she shook her head.

"Do you McLaughlins have mental telepathy with each other or something? This is getting a little ridiculous."

"Not telepathy, just got a call from my brother here." He gave his brother a hard look, before glancing back at Sarah. "What happened?"

"None of your business." She glared at Colin. "And I'm sure you broke some sheriff code by calling him."

Colin shrugged and gave a small grin. "I thought you might want help from an old friend. Ian owns a garage, you know."

The irritation on her face faded to surprise, and her gaze darted back to Ian. "No, actually I didn't know. I kind of figured he'd have a career dealing weed by now or something."

While Ian muttered a soft, "Ouch." His twin let out a roar of laughter.

"Well, it's legal now, so there are worse things," Colin murmured.

"Look, you guys can both take off. I'll call for a tow truck. Unless I'm getting some kind of ticket, Colin?"

"No. You swerved to avoid a deer and hit no other cars. Just...totaled your own. I think that's punishment enough."

Colin grimaced. "And I think you should consider getting checked out at the hospital."

Sarah waved off Colin's protest and turned, striding back to her car. "I'm fine. I just want to call my insurance and get things settled."

Ian thrust his hands into his jean pockets and followed her. "Go for it. But your insurance premium is going to go up."

"Why on earth would my insurance go up? This was an accident. I didn't cause it."

"Well, you did, actually. Colin just said you swerved to avoid hitting a deer?"

"Yes. Two, actually. One was a fawn. What are you getting at?"

"I'm saying that you swerved to avoid hitting a deer. Had you just braked instead of swerving, you wouldn't have been at fault."

"That makes no sense." She glanced at him over her shoulder. "Then I would've actually hit, and most likely killed, the deer. I would've felt awful, and my car would still be totaled. Are you even listening to yourself?"

"Look, I know what I'm talking about. My career is fixing cars, doll. I live on an island full of deer and have worked with insurance companies enough to know how this works. If you'd hit the deer, you would've been covered, because that wasn't your fault." He sighed. "But you swerved and made the choice to risk your life, meaning you caused the accident. It'll be an at-fault collision claim. Your rates are going to go up."

"Seriously? This is how life works? I decide to save Bambi and his mom and *I* get in trouble?"

Ian gave a slow laugh. "Pretty much. Next time just run them over and keep the meat."

Her nose wrinkled. "Okay, that's just horrible, not to mention gross."

"Aye." Ian frowned and took a step closer to her, concern sliding through him. Reaching out with the pad of his thumb, he caught the tiny trickle of blood just above her lip.

She sucked in a breath and pulled back. "What are—?"

"Your nose is bleeding. Did you hit the steering wheel?"

Her gaze locked with his and for a moment the world around them slowed and fell back in time. How many times had he stared into those eyes? Had his pulse been a little quick, just as it was now?

Maybe she felt it too, because she didn't look away and he heard the slight shift in her breathing. Then she blinked and her tongue darted out to wet her lips.

"I—I don't know if I hit my head. Honestly, I can't remember much except swerving. Then I saw red. The airbag went off though." Seeming almost self-conscious, she ducked her head and her hair slid forward in a curtain shielding her face.

Concern slid through him. "You should take Colin's advice and go to the hospital."

"I'll be fine."

He grunted in reply. "Still stubborn. Some things don't change."

"So what's your plan of action?" Colin called out as he approached again. "I've got a call coming in and need to go. Would you like me to send a tow truck?"

"Already called one for her on the way up," Ian answered before she could.

Her head jerked back up. "Wait, you did *what*?"

"Towing it to your garage then?" Colin confirmed.

"Aye."

"Right then. I'll be seeing you around, I'm sure, Sarah. Ian will have your car running in no time." With a wink at her and a nod at his brother, Colin disappeared back into his vehicle.

"Look, I'm not sure what kind of deal you and your twin have concocted here, but I'm not taking my car to your garage." Sarah's words were terse and her arms folded across her chest indicated her mind was made up.

"Ah. So you're filing a claim and picking another garage on the island then?"

She nibbled on her lip and uncertainty flickered across her face. "No. I'm not going to file a claim. I can't afford a spike in my insurance—I already have a speeding ticket from earlier in the year."

"Let me fix your car."

"Look, I can't afford to pay you," she blurted, and then

71

her cheeks flushed red. "I...I just don't have a lot of money right now."

He stared at her, knowing that had been damn hard for her to admit.

"I'm still paying attorney fees from the divorce."

Ah. Yes, that would certainly put a hole in one's finances. What did she even do for work now? He really didn't have any idea.

"Don't worry about it. I'm sure we can figure something out."

Her lips parted and her face lost a shade of color. Slowly she shook her head.

"Ian, that's probably not a good idea."

"No?" He arched a brow. "How do you intend to fix it then?"

"I don't know. But I don't want to be indebted to you. Don't you understand? I had no intention of even seeing you during this visit. This is a complete nightmare for me."

For some reason her impassioned—maybe unintentionally barbed—words hurt.

"Aye, I understand." His lips curved into a mocking smile, even as the urge to touch the tempting softness of her cheek suddenly overwhelmed him. Using his knuckles, he brushed a caress over the round apple of her cheek.

Touching her had always been his crack. Nothing had changed. He wanted to unwind that colorful scarf and expose the delicate skin of her neck. He could almost see the curve of her breasts between the folds of purple fabric.

There was so much he wanted. So much he'd be stupid to try and explore.

"Why is seeing me again so hard?" The question tore from him, quiet and confused. "Because of what happened?"

The panic across her face surprised him. So did the fact that she hadn't pushed his hand away.

"Please, let it go."

"For the moment, I suppose I'll have to." He glanced over her shoulder and noticed the tow truck pulling up in front of her wrecked car. "Just as it seems you'll have to accept my help."

THE RIDE TO his shop was only about five minutes, but in Sarah's mind it may as well have been an hour.

She was tucked into Ian's Camaro, speeding through the back roads of Whidbey Island. It was entirely too familiar. Too comforting—and she wasn't about to analyze why.

She'd held her breath more often than drawn one in. She just wanted to be invisible.

Right. A hysterical laugh—one that had been lingering for the last hour—built low in her throat. Of course she kept it restrained.

She closed her eyes again and drew in a slow breath. That didn't help in the least; instead it filled her nostrils with the smell of his soap. He'd never been a cologne guy, but she recognized the familiar soap he'd been so fond of buying from a local vendor on the island.

She'd been with him the first time he'd purchased it at a street fair. Beer soap, it had been touted. Not like it had smelled like a brewery or anything—it had been subtle, almost a faint nutty scent. But the word beer combined with soap had been just too cool for a teenage Ian. And apparently the grown Ian too.

She liked the smell, though. Always had. Unfortunately now it was bringing back too many memories.

The tires of the Camaro crunched over gravel, and she opened her eyes to see them arriving.

Who knew what she'd been expecting, but it wasn't this. The garage was located on the outskirts of Coupeville. A restored garage painted a vibrant blue. The words above the garage: *McLaughlin's Auto and Classic Car Restoration.*

Her lips fell open on a silent sigh. This wasn't a rundown auto shop by any means. Not the way she'd been expecting. It looked authentic. Tasteful. With a handful of employees working hard inside the garage.

"Here we are."

Unfastening her seat belt, she offered a grudging, "This looks like a nice place."

"That's because it is." His gaze met hers, and the hard glint in those amazing green eyes both captivated her and made her flinch. "Come on inside. I'll show you the place."

After a brief tour of the garage and meeting some of the

employees—all of whom seemed pretty nice—Ian took her into what appeared to be his office.

There was a door that locked and shutters that were closed. A computer sat on the desk, some kind of spreadsheet on the screen. She averted her gaze, but tried not to look at Ian either.

The office wasn't small, but it felt downright closet-sized with just the two of them inside it. Especially when he closed the door behind them.

Feeling his gaze on her—hot and heavy—she did her best not to squirm.

"So, how long have you had the garage?" *That probably sounded like the lame and obvious stall tactic that it was.*

"Six years." He moved toward her and her heart leapt into her throat. But he strode past her and dropped his keys on the desk instead. "Da fronted me the money to get it off the ground since the bank wouldn't lend to me."

"They wouldn't?" It didn't really surprise her all that much, though it did disappoint her a little.

"No. I didn't have the best credit history. And I'm sure the felony on my record didn't help."

Hearing him say the words aloud was a bit of a punch, and she could feel her eyes rounding. She'd known about the felony, but had always tried to not think about it. Wanted to believe it had been some kind of mistake.

Ten years ago she'd had a momentary lapse of sanity and had decided to try and contact Ian again. When her father had discovered what she was about to do, he'd presented her with Ian's latest background check—the felony conviction highlighted in yellow.

Ian seemed to be waiting for her shock and disgust. One brow was arched and his lips were curved into a slight smile, but his eyes were hard. They were always hard. As if the weight of the world, barbed and vicious, sat on his shoulders.

"Aren't you going to ask what the felony was?" His words were soft. His steps deliberate as he approached.

This time she knew his destination truly was her and not his desk.

"It's none of my business." The words came out on a croak.

I won't step back and let him think he scares me. No, it wasn't really him that scared her anyway, but her response to him.

"Second-degree assault," he answered anyway. "I beat a man nearly to death."

Bile churned in her stomach, and there was no disguising the shock in her eyes now. She blinked and jerked her gaze from him, staring instead at the wooden panels of the wall.

But along with the shock, there was such heavy sadness and disappointment.

"I'm not sure that gives you bragging rights."

"I'm not bragging, I'm warning you that I'm dangerous."

"You think I don't know that?" She gave a harsh laugh of disbelief and swung her attention back to him. "I tried to stay away from you, and yet you've dragged me back into your life."

He stood just inches from her, and despite her intent to stay strong, she wanted to scurry back another three feet. Put at least a bit of distance between them.

"You needed my help, doll. Which reminds me. We should talk payment."

Was this a joke? She'd already told him she was broke. "I don't have—"

"I don't want your money." He reached out, so quickly she hadn't seen his hand move, only felt it against her cheek.

Despite his large, calloused hands, his touch was surprisingly gentle. And it still had the ability to turn her body to mush. Made her mind a little foggy.

"I want a kiss."

Chapter Six

S HE BLINKED AND wet her lips. "W-what?"

"You heard exactly what I said." His gaze homed in on her mouth and his eyes darkened. "A kiss. It's not that complicated."

Oh, it was definitely that complicated.

"Not a chance."

"Why?"

"Are you high? Because we've got a history—a pretty complex one where I made it clear I wanted nothing to do with you. And beyond that, I'm not for sale, dammit."

Ian laughed. The sound so deep and sexy, she hated the way it heated her blood.

"I'm not asking you to suck me off. Though I sure as hell wouldn't protest if you tried. It's just a kiss."

The imagery. Oh, God, the imagery those words created. She shoved it aside, and sputtered, "You're disgusting. You kiss your mother with those lips?"

"Not since she moved back to Scotland with Da. And the only kissing I'd like to focus on is between you and I."

"It's not going to happen."

When she stepped back, he followed her. A deliberate dance of seduction. Of intimidation.

"It will happen, Sarah, because I want it to and I'm certain you do too."

"Arrogant much?" Her mouth went dry. "I was done with you the day I moved to Japan."

Okay, that was a lie. She'd never forgotten him—it would be impossible to. And each suggestive little sentence he uttered was turning her body to liquid heat. Which pretty much made her think she needed to have her head examined. Any normal woman would've reacted by slapping that smug smile off his face.

"And that's just the thing, doll. I wasn't done with you." His head dipped. "Not even close."

And before she could fire back a response, not that she had one after his explosive admission, he muttered, "I'm collecting my payment."

His mouth claimed hers.

Instinct demanded she fight him—push him away, but her mind reasoned that she could fight him another way. By not responding. By not giving him any indication that she still harbored any emotion except disdain for him.

But his kiss wasn't hard—wasn't aggressive. It was slow and sensual. Gentle even.

His mouth brushed over hers in a soft caress, again and again, before his tongue teased the seam of her pressed lips.

His shocking change of tactic tore down any walls she'd maneuvered between them. Emotions she'd thought long dormant stirred deep within her. Physical needs she hadn't realized she could experience anymore came to the surface.

The combination of the two was a bit terrifying.

She wasn't a twenty-eight-year-old woman anymore, but a seventeen-year-old with a stomach full of butterflies again.

The urge to part her lips, to kiss him back struck her with a ferocity that made her light-headed.

She slid her hands up his chest, clinging to his shirt to keep herself upright. Though there was no real danger of falling, not with the way he'd backed her up against the door.

Ian lifted his head a tiny bit. "You always were so damn sweet. Open your mouth for me, Sarah. I've got to taste you."

She shook her head.

"Do you want me to stop?"

Again, she shook her head, couldn't manage any reply except a small whimper. He used it. Once more his mouth took hers and his tongue slid past her parted lips. The moment his tongue touched hers the fight left her.

Just one more time, she bargained with herself. One more time to remember how good they'd once been.

Clinging to him now, she met the teasing flicks of his tongue with hesitant strokes of her own. Tasting him.

Heat and need spread through her blood like wildfire.

Catching and crackling, making every part of her come to life in a way that hadn't been matched in eleven years.

Pleasure exploded through her when he slid a large palm past her scarf and into the V neckline of her shirt. The sensation of his calloused hand cupping her breast had her nipple hardening instantly.

His growl of appreciation rumbled between them as he squeezed her flesh. He seemed to be eager to rediscover her shape and texture. His hand squeezed and lifted her breast; strong fingers swept in to pinch her nipple.

Sparks lit up in her head and she cried out, her knees most definitely buckling now.

So wrong. She knew it deep in her heart. This was so very wrong. It was nothing but lust at its deadliest. And because it had been so long since she'd experienced passion, she couldn't bring herself to push him away. Even with the reminder banging down her conscience at just how much was at stake. At how horribly he'd hurt her before.

An ache grew between her legs and she could feel her flesh slicken. The need made her want to do all kinds of crazy things. Hike up her skirt and just jump him. Wrap her legs around his waist—ignore the consequences—and just let her hormones rule her mind.

Right now she wasn't a stressed-out mom wondering how she was going to pay her rent and the lawyer. She was a woman who had needs that had been far too long ignored.

That's the only reason you're feeling like this. The voice of reason managed to infiltrate her cloud of lust, but it didn't make her pull away.

When Ian's mouth lifted from hers, she nearly pulled it back down, but then she realized where it was headed and moaned low in her throat.

He tugged the stretchy fabric of her top to the side and pulled the breast he'd been exploring free from her bra. His head swooped down, just before she felt the wet heat of his mouth close over her nipple.

A cry ripped from her throat and she arched into him, driving her fingers blindly into his hair.

So good.

Ian grabbed her waist with one hand, pulling her closer to him. Then she felt the nudge of his knee between her legs as he moved his other hand beneath her skirt and up her thigh.

He brushed his fingers over the heated flesh between her legs—was just starting to slip beneath her panties—when a loud pounding had him stilling.

"Hey, boss. Someone's here to see you," a muffled voice called through the door.

Ian lifted his head and locked gazes with her. The heat in his eyes made her mouth dry up.

She fully expected him to let her go and answer the door, but instead he slipped a finger beneath her panties and didn't even hesitate before he thrust it inside her body.

"Ian." She gave a strangled whisper of protest, and then

bit her lip hard enough to nearly draw blood so she wouldn't cry out in pleasure.

"Tell them to go the fuck away. I'm busy."

A knowing smile crossed his face, and he moved his finger higher, before locating her clit with ridiculous accuracy.

"Don't—"

One little pinch and he sent her over the edge. There was no stopping her sharp cry before Sarah buried her head against his shoulder to smother her moans as she rode out the waves of the small orgasm.

Dimly she heard, "Ugh, I don't think he's going away, boss. It's Curt MacGregor."

There was embarrassment in the employee's voice now. Oh yeah, he knew exactly what was going on. She would kill Ian later. Absolutely kill him. Or make him wish he were dead. At least once her body stopped trembling from the best orgasm ever.

Crap.

Floating back down to reality, she couldn't stop asking herself what the hell she had just done.

Curt MacGregor.

Ian didn't bother to stop the F-bomb that spilled from his lips. The name had the effect of a cold shower.

Dammit, this was not how he wanted this little moment to end. Not with his finger playing Sarah's clit like a guitar and his dick begging to be included in the action.

"I need to deal with this." Shuttering his expression, he moved away from her and pulled her skirt and top back into place.

"Give me two minutes and then show him in," he bit out tersely to Jack, who waited outside his office.

If Curt hadn't showed up, there was no doubt Ian would've taken Sarah in his office—probably against the door. They'd been minutes away from it, tops.

A quick glance at Sarah's face showed that she'd come down from cloud orgasm and was plotting the quickest way out of there. She wouldn't look at him as she busied herself fixing her scarf.

He clenched his jaw, trying not to think about how soft and sweet her breast had felt in his hand. His mouth. Because that sure wasn't helping his hard-on right now.

"Why don't you wait out front?" he said as she reached for the door handle a moment later. "We need to talk."

"Oh, I think we've talked enough. Or, funny, but *not* talked." She glared at him, her face flushed from embarrassment. Probably a little bit of remaining pleasure too.

"Sarah—"

"That was not *just a kiss*," she hissed, before scrambling out the door and slamming it shut behind her.

Fuck.

Irritation roared through him as he took a minute to compose himself in the bathroom in his office. When he came back out several minutes later, Curt was sprawled out on the couch.

MacGregor looked like he always did. Short, stocky, bald, and with an ugly mug, he kind of gave off a pit bull vibe. And the man still had an apparent aversion to personal hygiene, Ian realized as he approached him.

They'd met during Ian's brief stint in prison. Their connection had come from the fact they were both in on assault charges, and Curt had saved his arse—literally—within those first few days of Ian arriving at the pen.

They'd also bonded over both being Scottish. Though MacGregor had been in America since he was five and the States were all he'd ever really known. Ian's family had moved when he was fifteen. He was at the point where nearly half his life had been spent in Scotland, and half in America.

"MacGregor. How's it going?" Ian offered his hand, which the other man immediately reached out and slap-shook in greeting.

"It's going good. Real fucking good. Your garage is looking all classy-like now. I guess you're doing good too, huh, bro?"

Bro. At one point, during his three months in prison, he'd considered this man like another brother. But once out of prison and they'd both gone their separate ways, things had started to change.

Ian had made it a priority to get his life back on the right track. He couldn't regret the choice that had put him behind bars, but he could sure as hell try and get back on the straight and narrow road.

Curt, though, didn't seem so inclined.

"I've got some parts to sell you, if you're interested."

It wasn't even a question of being interested anymore. It had always just been an understanding that when Curt brought in car parts—some hard to find and expensive to order—Ian bought them. Under the table. No questions asked.

When he'd first opened the garage, he'd been a nobody and struggling just to stay open. He'd taken the risk and hadn't asked questions. But he'd had the garage for six years now and was starting to be well respected on the island. Some people might still whisper about his criminal record, but more overlooked it and accepted him.

Curt hadn't shown his face around here in nearly two years, and Ian had started to hope the other man had moved on. But here he was now, trying to pick up with business as usual.

"Nothing personal, MacGregor, but I think I'm going to pass."

Curt's grin hardened and dismay flickered in his eyes.

"What are you saying?"

Shite, there'd be no getting around it. "It's exactly how you pointed out. My garage *is* doing well, and I'm not sure I can be…" he paused and met Curt's gaze head on without flinching "…doing business with you anymore."

"Too good for me now, huh?" Curt gave a harsh, disbelieving laugh and smoothed a hand over his bald head.

A light, quick knock sounded on the door and Ian welcomed the interruption. He moved past Curt to open it.

Sarah stood on the other side. Her face was still slightly flushed, but she appeared a little more composed now. Even if she wouldn't look him in the eye.

She cleared her throat. "I forgot my purse."

Ian hid a smile. How far had she gotten before she'd realized? Had she even left the garage?

"This it?"

Ian and Sarah both glanced at Curt, and the strap of a black purse he swung around a beefy finger.

"Oh. Yes, thanks." Sarah hesitated, before stepping forward to retrieve it.

But Curt didn't immediately let go, instead he seemed to run an analytic glance over Sarah for a moment before relinquishing the purse.

"You're welcome, gorgeous."

Ian picked up immediately on the sudden tension in Sarah's stance and the flicker of discomfort across her face.

She glanced at Ian and there was wariness in her eyes now, but she didn't say anything. Instead, with a small nod at them both, she disappeared again.

"Isn't she a pretty little thing?"

Curt's light tone didn't fool Ian for a minute, and he

swore silently.

"She a friend of yours?"

"Don't know if I'd call her a friend. Old acquaintance really." He ground his teeth together and tried to keep his expression casual. He didn't want to give Curt any indication of how he really felt about Sarah.

Hell, not like he even really knew. He only knew he wanted to be buried inside her again, and that he'd never intentionally put her in harm's way. The fact that their parting had been bitter and painful was irrelevant.

He'd always kept Curt away from his family. Away from anyone who was important to him, because he wasn't all that sure he trusted the other man anymore. The brief world they'd shared while serving time didn't mix well into his current one.

"You should probably go, Curt."

Curt's attention whipped back to Ian. "I'm broke, bro. You need to help me out here."

"I can't do it anymore. I can't take that risk. This isn't just about me. I've got employees with families. I'm done."

"Fine. No problem." Curt stared at him for a moment and then cocked his head. "You know, that lady in here really was pretty cute. Maybe I should hang out on the island more. Get to know her."

Like hell. The son of a bitch was making a threat. A veiled one, but it was just as troubling. Curt had other friends too. Scary ones.

Flexing his jaw, Ian took a step toward the man he'd once considered such a close friend. It'd been an illusion. At the time he'd done what he'd had to do to survive.

"One last time, MacGregor. Come back after closing with the parts and I'll give you cash." He lowered his voice, not holding his punches. "But we're done after this, got it? You walk out of here tonight, and you're gone. You go do your own thing, and you stay away from the island."

Curt gave a slow nod, his eyes alight with realization. Shite, whether he'd meant to or not, Ian had tipped his hand to show Sarah was off limits. A weak spot for him.

"No problem, bro." Curt grinned and turned to leave. "See you later tonight."

∽

"AND DONE." SARAH saved the changes she'd just made on the website for her client and then pulled up her email on her laptop.

It felt good to work. Oh dear God, she really did need the distraction.

This afternoon she'd lost her mind. There was no denying it. Because even though she'd been in the powerful haze of passion, she'd known *exactly* what she was doing.

She'd gotten all hot and heavy with Ian. With the man who had shattered her heart so badly she didn't think it would ever be able capable of love again.

She'd tried to be open to the possibility of falling in love again in Japan. Had hoped it would happen when she married Neil, but it had barely taken any time at all before she'd come to face the ugly reality. He wasn't Ian, he would never be Ian, and her heart still belonged to a man an ocean away.

Unfortunately Neil had realized that pretty early on too. And it hadn't settled well.

Closing her eyes against the wave of anxiety and sadness, she swallowed the lump in her throat.

She was in a better place now. Absolutely. It didn't matter that she was struggling financially and going it alone. There was still one person who she loved beyond measure. Her daughter. Emily was her world. Her heart.

And she was stupid, ridiculously stupid—and apparently ridiculously horny—to have tried to throw it all away. To have risked everything for an orgasm from Ian.

But, oh, what an orgasm it had been.

"No," she muttered, standing up. "It was a really bad lapse in judgment. And it won't happen again."

It couldn't happen again. Her conviction had only grown when she'd stepped back into the office to grab her purse. Whoever Ian had been talking to gave off the vibe that he'd just crawled out from under a rock.

Unease had spread through her the minute she'd seen him, and the thorough look-over he'd given her had made her skin crawl.

She'd immediately sensed he wasn't a kind person, or

someone she'd want in her life in the slightest. And yet he seemed to be friends with Ian. Doing business with him.

Which was why she was going to keep her distance from Ian. No more kisses as bargains—what the hell had that been about anyway? Ian hated her, probably almost as much as she hated him.

How close hate and love were woven, though.

Needing to jump back into her distraction, she opened another project on her computer.

Actually, it was getting late, and a glass of wine sounded kind of awesome. She stood and went to the kitchen to open the bottle she'd just bought at the grocery.

The walk to the small store hadn't taken too long, an hour tops there and back. The last thing she'd wanted to do was ask Ian to take her in his car, so since it was a beautiful day she'd thrown on her walking shoes and headed out.

After removing the cork from the budget bottle of wine, she grabbed a glass from the cupboard. Her gaze caught on a movement outside the window and she made a strangled sound of disbelief.

And here he was again. Ian McLaughlin, strolling up Gran's drive like it was completely natural and expected.

Chapter Seven

S HE REACHED THE front door before Ian could knock and she swung it open.

"Have you decided to become my shadow? Why don't you just run on home?" She arched a brow. "I'm assuming you have one?"

Ian gave a small smile, but it didn't reach his eyes. "I'm renting a house down in the Greenbank area. Can I come in?"

She absorbed that little tidbit of knowledge, and sighed. "That's probably a bad idea."

"But you're going to let me in anyway?" He continued onto the porch and then stepped right over the threshold.

Once again, her space shrank to just the two of them. Her head went light with the scent of him, and when his body brushed hers as he entered, her breath caught.

"You don't take the word no very seriously, do you?" she muttered, and shut the door behind him.

"Actually, I do." His jaw hardened, his eyes clouded. "It carries a lot of weight with me."

He was serious, she realized. There was more than just words there.

"Are you having a bit of wine?" He nodded to the open bottle. "Would you mind if I have a glass?"

"I'd rather you didn't. I'm not even sure why you've come by. I'm hoping you won't be here long."

"Fair enough." He thrust his hands into his pockets. "I won't be here longer than necessary. I promise."

She hesitated a moment before going to grab another glass and pouring him a little bit as well.

"Thank you." He took the glass and lifted his gaze to hers. "We should talk about your car."

"Yes, we should. I've decided I'm going to try and take cash out on my credit card and pay you."

"That won't be necessary. I don't need your money."

"Yes, well, I'd rather not owe you any more kisses." She could feel her cheeks burning hot. "Or whatever other tawdry payment you're expecting."

"I expected nothing. The kiss was…" he hesitated "…hell, I don't know where that idea came from. Only that it seemed like a good idea at the time."

"How is kissing me a good idea? We have an awful history, and you have a girlfriend. Though I guess it's never stopped you before."

"Ouch. Another low blow."

"Not that low."

He grunted. "Gina's not my girlfriend. It was more of a

hooking-up thing. And that's over."

"Is it?" Right. Hookup or not, that woman on his arm this afternoon had been ten times sexier than she was.

There was resolve in his eyes as he answered. "Yes. I plan to call her later, actually."

And she believed him. It probably made her stupid as hell, but she believed him. Had she learned nothing?

Bitter with the realization, she took another sip of wine.

"And our history wasn't all horrible."

Her heart clenched. Why didn't he just drop it? Why was he so determined to try and deepen a scar that would never disappear?

"The end was horrible. It kind of taints the rest, don't you think?"

"I don't really know. I have a hard time forgetting the rest sometimes." A bitter smile twisted his mouth. "Much harder than you it seems."

She watched him take another sip of wine. Saw the bead of red gather on his lip and had to fight the temptation to lean forward and kiss it away.

If someone would've told her ten years ago that Ian would be standing here, saying these kinds of things and seeming almost vulnerable, she would've laughed.

Ian was a born and bred bad boy. His agenda in life seemed to be to have fun and screw the consequences. Early on, maybe that first time they'd met in the car, he might've even said that to her.

He hadn't changed, though. And she couldn't afford to get involved with him again. It was a risk to so much more than her heart.

Hardening her resolve, and any romantic side of her that was screaming, "*Maybe…*" she stepped away from him and moved into the living room.

The upholstered couch had to be two decades old at least, and it showed the wear and love from the years. She sank into it, breathing in the familiar scent of Gran's house that rose with the dust.

"I need to get some work done tonight. So why don't you finish up with what you came to tell me, and we'll call it a night?"

WHAT HE CAME to tell her? Ian bit back a sharp laugh of disbelief. Hell, he wasn't quite sure what he'd come to tell her. Maybe, no definitely, warn her to stay away from MacGregor if she saw him anywhere.

But first, he had to get her off the idea of paying him for repairing the car. She'd already admitted she was broke, and he truly had no need for her money. His reputation was fantastic and his clientele was expanding by the week. Sure, he did simple car repairs on the island, but word had spread about the work he did on classic car restoration. He was the garage people on—and off—the island came to.

"Tell you what," Ian began, "instead of kisses, instead of

money, why don't we—"

The ringing of her cell phone had him trailing off. Maybe it was a good thing because he wasn't quite sure what'd he'd been about to offer.

"Shouldn't you answer that?" he asked, when Sarah made no move to answer her cell. "What if it's your daughter?"

"It is," she admitted, and seemed reluctant to answer. "Give me a moment."

He watched her answer the phone. Her tone and expression softened as he listened to the tender conversation with her daughter.

As if she couldn't take his gaze on her anymore, she stood and paced in front of the window as she chatted.

Ian took her place on the couch, sipping his wine as he stared out the large window behind her. The view was rather spectacular. You could see part of the historic town of Coupeville, and then beyond it the small inlet of saltwater named Penn Cove—famous for the mussels grown there.

Even though it was heading toward six in the evening, there were still sailboats and kayakers out. No doubt enjoying the longer days of summer and awaiting the upcoming sunset.

"Sorry about that." Sarah hit a button on her cell phone and came to sit down again. "She's on the east coast and is just getting ready for bed. She wanted to call and say goodnight. We've never been apart this long, and I know it isn't easy for her. Or me. At bedtime I usually tuck her in and have her read out loud to me from a chapter book."

"That's quite sweet." And it was. He didn't have much experience with kids—none of his siblings had any yet. But he knew when the time came, he could probably adapt slowly to the uncle role. "What did you say her name was?"

"I didn't, but it's Emily."

"Pretty. How old is she?"

"She's eight. Almost nine." Sarah tucked her phone back into her purse. "I'm sorry, now what were you saying before she called? Something about payment for my car?"

"Ah yes, I was." What the hell had he been about to offer? "Why don't you just bake us muffins or something?"

The look Sarah threw at him could've frozen ice. "I'm sorry? Bake muffins?"

"Er, you don't have to. It was just a suggestion. You weren't overtly fond of the kissing one—"

"I'm not. No more kisses." Her mouth flattened into a line of determination.

He laughed softly and arched a brow. "I think you enjoyed it, doll. And before you try to claim otherwise, remember I was there when you were riding out an orgasm on my finger."

Her choked gasp coincided with the widening of her eyes. "You're awful. You had to say that? Really?"

His laugh turned to a belly one now. Loud and resounding in the room. "It'd be more unnatural if I didn't."

"Well then get a filter for your thoughts. Most people

have one."

"Hmm. I'll keep it in mind, but it's not quite as fun." He sobered some and lifted his gaze to hers again. "But I truly don't need your money, Sarah. Keep it. I'll do this as a favor."

"I don't want any favors from you."

"Well you've got one anyway. You don't really need to bake muffins. I was taking the piss out of you."

"What?" Her brows furrowed.

"Sorry, I'll Americanize that for you since you clearly need a reminder on the phrase. I was *messing with you*."

She made another harrumph.

"You said you had to work. What do you do for a living? It obviously travels well."

"I'm a graphic designer. Most of my business is online."

"And it pays shite?"

"No, it pays pretty good when the business is coming in."

He paused, taking another sip of wine, before asking, "But you're broke?"

"Not usually. It's the legal fees from the divorce, and I've had to drop some clients because of the time it's been taking up." She shook her head and gestured around the house. "This time here will actually be good for me. I'm able to take on more clients—if I can get them. I'm still new. I only just completed college."

"Which you're also paying off?"

"Yes."

"Understood." Why had she waited so long after high school? Had getting married and having a kid slowed that dream down?

Aleck had hounded him to go to college and get a degree after graduation. Told him to pull his head out of his arse and stop crying over a woman and focus on his life. On his future.

And so he had. Granted, school had been spread out because he'd had to serve a tiny stint in prison, but he'd eventually graduated with a degree in business.

Maybe Sarah had attended college for a bit and then dropped out because she'd become pregnant.

The thought of Sarah with another man—a husband who'd given her a child—made the wine turn bitter in his belly.

He'd mastered the ability to turn his thoughts from Sarah when they appeared. And forget thinking about Sarah and a husband. Literally, he couldn't think about the reality of it without feeling ill—even a bit violent toward the other man, actually.

He set his wine down on the coffee table next to the couch and stood.

"I should go.

"A fabulous idea," she said over brightly. "Thanks for dropping by, Ian."

"Before I do, though, I wanted to warn you about Mac-

Gregor."

She tilted her head, though he saw the flicker of aware-ness in her eyes. "MacGregor?"

"The man you saw me speaking to in my office?"

"Ah, yes."

Judgment clouded her gaze now, and he knew she was again finding his choice in company disappointing. He couldn't blame her. It didn't matter, though, this was too important. This was about keeping her safe.

"Stay away from him," he said with quiet authority. "Please."

She looked skeptical and gave a nervous laugh. "It's not as if I planned to go have a beer and burger with the guy. He's not my type in the least."

"I realize that. What I'm saying is if you do see him around, give him a wide berth. Stay away. And let me know immediately."

She swallowed visibly, wariness flickering in her eyes now. "What kind of guys do you run with? And why are you dragging me into their circle?"

"I never intended to drag you in." Whether he'd intend-ed to or not, he had. And he was kicking himself over the realization. "Your paths crossed, unfortunately, and it's not something I can undo. I just wanted you to be warned."

"Your friends sound awesome. Just awesome."

He'd have to be dead to miss her sarcasm.

Ignoring her words, and denying how much they stung,

he dug in his pocket for the card he'd stuffed there earlier.

"Here's the info for the garage. I put my personal cell number on the back if you need anything."

"I won't." But she took it anyway.

"Careful. Because you might." He went to the front door and paused. "Thanks for the wine, doll. And sorry about the kiss."

She rolled her eyes and folded her arms across her chest. "You're not sorry."

His lips twitched. "No, I can't say that I am. And neither are you."

～

SARAH WATCHED HIM go. Her heart was pounding a little too fast and there were butterflies in her stomach. They were the same damn symptoms she'd had all those years ago. Symptoms that warned she could fall for him all over again if she wasn't careful.

And she had to be careful. She had to be *very*, very careful.

She refused to end up in the same boat she'd been in eleven years ago…

～

"WE'RE MOVING TO Japan." The words she'd been dreading were out. Fleeing her mouth on a wave of emotion and tears that she couldn't let fall. "My dad got his orders and he's getting stationed there."

Ian stared at her. Absolute shock registering on his face. "No. You can't go."

Misery welled in her and she shrugged. "I don't want to, but I don't think I have a choice. I'm not eighteen yet."

"You will be in a year."

"Yeah. A year." Tears did flood her eyes now.

"Can't you stay here? If we talk to my parents, I'm sure they'd take you in. They love you." Ian's voice grew more animated with the idea. "You and Kenzie can share a room—"

"You don't understand. *My* dad hates you. He's thrilled that this move will break us up. He says I need a year, at least, to make sure you're really what I want out of life."

Ian pulled her into his arms, his voice low as he asked, "And you think I am?"

"I know you are," she whispered. "I'm not going to lie. I want to go to college after graduation and get a degree, but I love you. I don't think I'll ever love anyone like I love you. We can take it slow, but there's no one else I want."

"Then we'll make it work, doll." He kissed her forehead again, then the tip of her nose, and finally her mouth. "Trust me. I'll go talk to your dad tonight."

She gave a soft harrumph, only half-kidding as she advised, "You might want to wear a bulletproof vest."

Ian laughed, though, and tightened his arms around her. "We'll just be real with him. He's got to know how we feel about each other."

"He knows. I just don't think he cares." She sighed. "What time does your party start tonight?"

"Eight. Are you sure you don't want to come?"

"I don't drink." She wrinkled her nose. "Besides. This is for the graduating seniors—I'd feel like a dork crashing it."

"You're my girlfriend. No one's going to question you being there with me."

No one would question it because she'd be on Ian McLaughlin's arm. His reputation still ensured that people weren't stupid enough to start something with him. Ian was right. Her presence might be bitched about quietly, but wouldn't dare be voiced aloud.

"Besides, Hailey and Steve are going," she added. "She'll keep an eye on you."

Ian and Sarah had often gone on double dates with the other couple. Hailey was another cheerleader and a close friend on the cheerleading squad.

"What, you don't trust me?" he teased.

"You know I do," she said softly. "I just get nervous with a lot of intoxicated teenagers."

"You sound like my mother." He kissed her again. "I promise I won't have more than a few beers."

"You'd better not, because that's an MIP. If you get caught."

"Never been caught before."

"It's really kind of disturbing the things you brag about," she drawled.

"I'm not bragging."

Though she enjoyed teasing him, she knew he wasn't all that big of a drinker. Sure, he and his friends snuck a few beers or Scottish whisky now and then, but they never got totally wasted.

It had bothered her at first, more so because she was such a rule follower. She refused to drink until the government told her she legally was of age to do so. But she was also aware that if she refused to date any guy that drank underage, the pickings were slim.

And she didn't really want to pick anyway. Ian was her soul mate. She knew it, without a doubt. The bad boy act was just that. More for show than a reality. It was an image he projected to the world, and she still wasn't sure why. But then, they'd only been dating for seven months.

"I should go. I need to study for a chemistry final on Monday." She sighed and snuggled closer. "But promise you'll be careful tonight, okay?"

"I promise. You want to grab breakfast tomorrow?"

Yes. "Sure you won't be too hungover?" she asked lightly.

"Do I have to say it again? I'm not getting drunk."

"Okay, then I'd love to. I just heard how crazy these end-of-the-year senior parties are."

"Well you don't need to worry about me. I'll text you by nine."

He kissed her again, deeper this time, and her heart and head spun in a giddy swirl of love and happiness.

"Can't wait," she whispered when he lifted his head.

AND THAT HAD been the last time everything had been sunshine and roses between them. It had gone to hell in a handbasket pretty damn fast when morning came.

The visual slipped through her head. The memory of wandering through the party house, trying to find Ian. And then when she had...

Not wanting to think about it anymore, she started to re-cork the wine when another knock sounded on her door.

Had Ian come back?

Groaning in disbelief, she went to peek through peephole to be safe.

She had the door open in seconds. "Hey, you. I'm trad-ing one McLaughlin for another tonight."

Chapter Eight

KENZIE ARCHED A brow, the same damn way Ian did all the time, and stepped into the house.

"Which brother of mine has been here? Or do I really need to ask?"

Crap, maybe she shouldn't have let that comment about trading McLaughlins loose.

"Never mind, I don't have to ask. The blush on your face says it all." Kenzie strode into the kitchen. "I see you've got the wine going already. Good, because I've brought dinner. Aleck sent me with a couple shepherd's pies, chips and another apology."

"Oh yum. Tell him apology accepted, with or without the pies." She snagged the brown bag from her friend and peeked inside, inhaling the scent of meat and gravy. "Though the pies are definitely helping."

"I know, right? So why was Ian here?" Kenzie's tone was deceptively light as she grabbed a wineglass and poured herself some. "You want some?"

"No thanks, I've still got a bit left from earlier." Sarah

pulled the shepherd's pies from the bag and began to unwrap them. "Ian was, um, was working out a payment for my car."

"What happened to your car?"

"You didn't hear?" Sarah cast her a quick glance as she found plates. "I assumed you would've. Both Colin and Ian showed up at the scene to help me."

"No, I didn't hear. Scene? Did you get in a crash?" Alarm wove through Kenzie's rising voice. "Are you hurt?"

"I'm fine. I swerved to avoid a deer and ran off the road and hit a tree."

"You're so lucky you're okay. You should've just hit the deer."

"Exactly what your brother said." Sarah grimaced and carried the plates to the dining room.

"And your insurance will say so too." Kenzie followed her and took a seat.

"He said that as well. Which is why I'm not calling them to file a claim."

"So Ian's fixing your car?"

"Yeah."

"I hope he gave you a good deal." Kenzie paused to take a bite, but her gaze stayed on Sarah. "You're blushing again."

"He's not charging me."

"Well now. That *is* a good deal."

"Yes." Sarah diverted her attention and focused on her food. It was much easier burying her head and focusing on nearly orgasmic shepherd's pies from the McLaughlin Pub.

"Ian's not a bad guy you know…"

Kenzie obviously had no clue of the type of guys Ian did business with. But she obviously knew her brother was a felon. How could Kenzie even try to deny that her brother was the type a smart girl stayed clear of?

"Maybe while you're here you guys could let the past go and give it another chance? It's clear there's still some chemistry between you both."

Sarah fell back against her chair, shock roiling through her. "Holy crap. You did *not* just say that."

"Why, because he made an awful mistake? We all do. He's not perfect."

Sarah made a soft snort. "He's nowhere near perfect. Besides, Ian and I were ages ago. I've moved on."

"Have you? Because I see the way you look at him. And that doesn't scream 'moved on' to me."

With her heart pounding now and despondency clawing at her throat, Sarah shook her head. "Please, I'd rather not talk about it."

"Fine. Sorry, you're right. I'm being ridiculous. Of course there's not a chance for reconciliation there." Kenzie gave a chagrined shrug. "I'm afraid I've always been reluctant to let go of the idea of you as a sister-in-law."

Yes. It had been the topic at so many slumber parties, or during coffee runs made before first period. Kenzie had always been thrilled with Sarah and Ian dating.

"So tell me about Neil. I didn't even know you'd gotten

married until you emailed me months later."

"Sorry, yeah. It was all very low key." The food she was eating began to taste like sawdust as thoughts of her ex-husband filtered into her mind. "We met when I was almost twenty. He was just a few years older than me. A sailor my dad worked with and introduced me to."

"Right, I remember you said he was in the navy. Well you certainly bounced back from Ian well enough."

Ouch. Ouch a hundred times over. Though she knew Kenzie hadn't meant to be accusing or anything, just conversational.

"But it didn't work out between you guys, huh? I'm sorry."

I'm not. "Sometimes you're better off alone."

"Oh, trust me. I understand." Kenzie's forehead furrowed as she continued to eat. "I think I've resigned myself to being single, but I'll be all right."

"I don't know how you're single." Sarah shook her head, truly confused. "You've always had guys trailing you around like lovesick puppies. Men love you."

Something like pain flashed in Kenzie's eyes—and maybe something darker. Fear? Before she shrugged. "They love the idea of me. Or just my body."

She wanted to ask her friend to elaborate, but then Kenzie laughed and her expression turned light once more. "We sure know how to turn the topic to the heavy stuff, aye?"

"Aye." Sarah couldn't help but grin and mimic Kenzie

good-naturedly.

"You said something about movies? Am I going to have to turn on Lifetime? Or do you have something good floating around?"

"Pretty sure Gran has some classics."

"*Singin' in the Rain*? We watched it with her once when we came over for pizza, I remember. I'd totally watch that again."

Sarah remembered that day too. Her lips curled fondly. Gran had been awesome to come hang out with. She'd even brought Ian over on several occasions for dinner.

Standing from the table, she murmured, "Well, I'm sure we can find it around here somewhere. Let's watch it again."

∾

IAN LAY IN bed, staring at the slow-moving ceiling fan since sleep was evading him.

His thoughts wouldn't stop going a mile a minute. And every last one of them had to do with Sarah.

Just thinking about what had happened in his office had his dick stirring once more. He'd struggled to not walk around with a hard-on the rest of the day.

And tonight, it still lingered. He knew before he fell asleep, he'd likely take matters into his own hands. Literally.

Though his arousal had tapered somewhat after the sour conversation with Gina. She'd not been happy in the slightest to learn he was moving on.

But it wasn't fair to her. Not that she'd wanted serious, but now he couldn't even give her casual. Not with Sarah on the island.

Gina hadn't taken the phone call well. And had cursed him to hell and back, vowing to head out to another bar in town and take home the first biker she could find. If she'd been hoping to make him jealous, she'd failed.

If anything, he hoped she would do exactly that. Perhaps it would help her move on quicker. He worried that she might've gotten a bit attached, despite protests otherwise.

His thoughts returned to Sarah. Again. He remembered the feel of her lips beneath his, and he made a murmur low in throat.

Bollocks. What was wrong with him?

He wasn't seriously entertaining the idea of trying to re-kindle something with her again, was he?

No. Perhaps he could seduce her into some short-term island fun, where no emotions beyond lust were involved. But anything serious was out of the question. He would never be good enough for Sarah. Not in his eyes, and certainly not in hers.

Closing his eyes, he remembered how everything had gone from so perfect, to so completely fucked up.

"HAVE ANOTHER WHISKY, Ian. You brought it."

He shook his head, even as his glass was topped off by

some guy he recognized from gym. Shite, when Da discovered he'd snatched the bottle from the pub, he was going to have kittens.

The music at the party blared, and nobody seemed to worry since the kid throwing the party lived out in the middle of the woods with no neighbors for miles. His parents, both doctors, were in Seattle for a medical conference.

"Are you having fun?" Hailey appeared at his side, a shot glass in her hand.

"Aye, it's a good party."

"Hell yeah it is." She bumped her glass into his. "Cheers."

"Cheers."

They drank their shots together.

She set her glass down and hiccupped. Her cheeks were red and her eyes were glassy.

"You're completely pissed, aren't ya?"

Hailey frowned, pushing back a wayward strand of chestnut hair. "What? No, I'm not mad."

He grinned. "Not mad. Drunk."

She gave a wide grin that flashed a dazzling smile, and propped a hand on her hip. "Oh. Yeah, I think I'm a little drunk."

And a bit adorable too. Big brown eyes that seemed almost doe-like. She wasn't much taller than Sarah, but quite pale and a little on the scrawny side. Her clothes weren't as fashionable as some of the other girls' at the party, but she looked pretty in the short blue lace dress.

He knew her family struggled with money. Actually, rumor had it her parents were crackheads and she was just trying to graduate and get off the island.

And Sarah had told him she was able to stay on the cheerleading squad from a scholarship. Sarah had befriended her early on—taken her under her wing, so to speak. There weren't many weekends where Kenzie, Sarah and Hailey weren't sleeping over at Sarah's house. Sometimes Kenzie had them over, though, and he loved those nights. He'd always manage to sneak Sarah away for a few stolen kisses.

But they were tight-knit friends, the three of them.

"So is Steve the designated tonight?" He glanced around the crowded room, trying to pinpoint Hailey's boyfriend.

"No. Steve went to some party in Anacortes." She hesitated. "Actually, we broke up a couple days ago."

"Shite, really? I'm sorry. Sarah didn't say anything about it."

"I didn't tell her. I'm still in shock." Hailey's cheeks, already red from alcohol, flushed further. "He dumped me for some college chick at Western."

Christ, his gender could suck.

"But enough about me and my shitty love life," Hailey continued, a bit bitterly. "Want another drink?"

He mentally calculated how many he'd had. Three? Or four? "I'm actually good."

"Just one more. Then you can tell me where you're going to school next year."

He didn't have the heart to turn her down when she returned with a beer.

An hour later, when Hailey ran off to use the bathroom, he took the time to call Sarah and tell her how much he loved her. Asked her if she'd pick him up in the morning, since Colin had needed to borrow his car.

He knew the call likely fell into the drunken dialing category, and he'd tried to keep his voice from slurring. Because one beer had turned into two. Or was it three? Hailey had just kept bringing them to him—and those were on top of the shots.

They'd ended up on the deck outside, talking about colleges. About Sarah and how perfect she and Ian were together. The music had been good, the crowd positive.

He lost count of the drinks she'd given him, but he must've had more than he'd thought, because he was starting to feel pretty tired. Dizzy.

Shite, he hoped he didn't make an arse of himself and throw up on anyone.

He excused himself and stumbled to the bathroom, but when he spotted an open bedroom door, the temptation to lie down on the empty bed for a moment was overwhelming.

Falling onto the mattress, he closed his eyes.

"Ian?" The soft voice seemed to be miles away.

The bed dipped and he felt a warm, female body next to

him.

Sarah?

"You're so sweet to me," she whispered and wrapped an arm around his waist.

Did her lips brush his neck? Did he kiss her next? It was hard to tell. It was all becoming a blur as he followed her down the dark path into oblivion.

The next thing he knew someone was calling his name.

"Ian?"

The voice, soft and hesitant, pulled him from the dark void. Ian struggled to open his eyes, and when his lids finally opened, he was blinded by the sunlight pouring into the room.

"Ian?" The questioning, female voice grew closer.

He struggled to sit up, realized the weight of something was weighing him down. Or someone.

Shock slammed through him as became aware of the soft body curled up next to his. Naked—just as naked as he was. And the woman wasn't Sarah, but one of her best friends.

No. Shite, *no* this wasn't happening.

"Are you in here?" There was a soft knock on the door.

"Wait," he rasped, trying to ease away from Hailey.

But the door twisted open and Sarah's head ducked inside.

"There you—" The color leeched from Sarah's face as she took in the scene.

"Sarah, wait."

"*Oh my God.*" Her voice rose now.

"It's not—"

"What it looks like? How can it not be?" she choked out, eyes wide with horror and tears. "And is that *Hailey?*"

Hailey, who'd been out for the count, stirred at the sound of her name. And then quickly came awake and sat upright.

The sheet fell from her, exposing a breast and slamming another nail into the coffin of guilt against him.

She'd climbed into bed with him. Had been all over him. That much he remembered. After that, not so much.

This wasn't happening. How could he have been so stupid? How could he have fallen back into the selfish, uncaring bastard that he'd been before Sarah?

"Sarah," he muttered thickly, not even sure what he could say. "I love you. You've got to know—"

"That you're a horrible, horrible person?" she ground out, silent tears running down her face. "Yes, I can see that. I think I always knew it, but got caught up in whatever illusion you were projecting to get me into bed. To think I mistook lust for love."

Ian shoved himself out of bed, not giving a damn about nudity anymore. "You know that's never how it was."

"Apparently, what I thought I knew was all crap. You're exactly like my dad always said. Worthless. I'm only sorry it took something like this to make me realize it."

He caught her arm when she tried to run, swinging her back into the room. Her fists plowed into his shoulders and she let out a sob.

"You don't mean that, doll."

"Don't *doll* me. It's a good thing you're great in bed, Ian, because that's about all you've got going for you in life. Good luck turning screwing into a career."

From the bed, Hailey made a small gasp of dismay, but Ian couldn't think about her now. Could only think of how he could possibly calm Sarah down. Help her understand...but, fuck, understand what? He couldn't even understand why he'd done what he'd done. Why he'd throw away everything to sleep with another chick he wasn't even attracted to.

"Sarah, take a breath. We can talk rationally when you've calmed down."

"Don't even try and placate me. You're a pathetic excuse for a human." She was in a full-on rage now. Crying and trembling, struggling to free her wrist from his grip. "You know what? I'm surprised you even made it through high school, but you're never going to get anywhere in life."

Ouch. Holy hell, but that had hurt. Everything she was saying hurt.

"Aye?" He nodded slowly. "That's how you've always felt, isn't it?"

She lifted her chin. "Pretty much, I just spent too long trying to tell myself you'd change."

With a sheet wrapped around her, Hailey approached the two of them. "Sarah, please. I know you're upset, but—"

"There *is* no 'but' that could possibly excuse this." Sarah turned her fury, her pain on the other woman. "You're one of my best friends. Or you were until you slept with my boyfriend."

"I'm so sorry," Hailey whispered, and there was genuine regret in her voice. Tears.

"Save it for someone who cares, because from this point on I don't." Sarah jerked away from Ian, stumbling toward the door.

"Don't leave like this."

She shook her head, but hesitated at the door. "There will never be anyone more important in your life than you. You're a selfish asshole. You're *nothing*, Ian, and will always be nothing. To me and to everyone else."

He couldn't even move now, couldn't bring himself to try and argue. The desperation and despondency had begun to fade, and the hardened part of him that was damned good at surviving rose to the surface.

He wasn't proud of the way he let his expression become almost mocking as she stared him down one last time. But it was the only way he knew how not to break. And she was damn close to breaking him.

He forced a crooked smile. "Well now, I'm sure it's a relief to have that off your chest."

"You can go to hell," Sarah whispered. "Both of you."

And then she'd fled the house.

IAN OPENED HIS eyes and stared at the ceiling fan again,

bringing himself back to the present. Out of the painful memory.

Every word Sarah had spat at him that day had been like toxic darts, burying deep into his body and poisoning his soul. Killing any shred of decency he'd had left.

He'd known he'd screwed up, and good, but he couldn't have been prepared to see her sweet demeanor fade into such hate and spite. The way she'd finally stripped away the fluffy outer shell to show exactly how she felt about him. How she'd probably always felt about him, while she'd just been indulging her wild side with a bad boy.

He was nothing. Would never be anything.

How much of a class fool did it make him to have thought she'd seen him differently? To think she'd brought out another side of him to the point where he'd begun to think it was possible to change.

He'd been fooling himself as much as her.

When she'd left the party house, he'd had every intention of giving her a few days to cool off before trying to talk to her again. Trying to smooth things over, at least to the point where maybe they could be friends.

Because the idea of losing her completely had been almost a physical pain. And yet within a week she'd been gone. Hadn't returned to school and then the whispers came that she'd moved to Japan with her family.

And then moving on with his life was the only choice he had.

Chapter Nine

"SO WHAT ARE you up to?"

Cradling her cell phone between her ear and shoulder, Sarah stared at the computer screen and pondered Kenzie's question.

"Well, I'm going to try and get some work done."

"Hmm. Will that take you the entire day?"

"Not all day, but several hours likely." Sarah sighed and leaned back in the chair. "Okay, out with it. What's going on?"

"It's just that you haven't left your house in two days." Kenzie's voice gentled. "There's a great band coming in to the pub tonight, and you should drop by."

Sarah sighed and lifted her gaze to the view outside the living room window. A night in the pub both tempted and scared the hell out of her.

She craved human contact and had never been the type who liked to spend great amounts of time alone. The evening with Kenzie watching movies had been perfect. They'd talked about high school and they'd laughed—they'd laughed so hard they'd cried at times, but they hadn't discussed Ian again.

And though she wanted to see Kenzie again tonight, the idea of seeing Ian made everything inside her chest go tight.

"Sarah, it's just not healthy turning yourself into a recluse."

"I'm not a recluse. I just have to work."

"Not every minute of the day. Come in tonight."

Sarah clutched the phone and closed her eyes. "I don't know if I can handle seeing him again."

"I understand." Kenzie's tone softened. "We all do. But you're going to be here for a month. You guys need to get past this. Or at least form a truce."

A truce. Maybe that's what Sarah could call it when she had allowed him to stick his tongue into her mouth again. Among the other things he'd done to her. She hadn't breathed a word about what had happened between her and Ian to Kenzie. Didn't want to encourage her.

"Drop by for an hour at least. If you're not comfortable, head out. Plus, there's no guarantee Ian will even come into the pub tonight."

"But there's a chance," Sarah protested.

"Of course there's a chance. Aleck may own the pub now, but our family is still a huge part of it. It's who we are."

"Aleck owns the pub?"

"Aye. Da sold it to him when he and Ma moved back to Scotland."

Sarah remembered the story of the McLaughlins. How Brenda McLaughlin had been an American citizen backpacking Europe, when she'd met and married Rodrick McLaughlin in Scotland. After several years and four children, the couple had moved the family to Whidbey Island in the United States. That was almost fifteen years ago. But now it seemed the parents had moved back to Scotland.

She'd missed so much in the last eleven years. Her heart ached when she thought of Kenzie's parents. They'd been like second parents to her. She had secretly dreamt of them being her in-laws.

God, she'd been so naïve at seventeen. So idealistic.

"Please say you'll come in. I'm singing too."

That caught Sarah's attention. "You're singing?"

"Aye. I join the band on stage now and then." Kenzie laughed. "There's no need to sound so shocked. I've got a decent voice."

"You do. I remember when we'd be on the bus to go cheer at a game, you used to always be singing." Sarah laughed. "We couldn't shut you up, actually."

"Ah, well now you need to come in tonight. You deserve a kick in the arse for that comment."

"I do." Sarah hesitated only a moment longer. "Fine, I'll come in."

"Good. Band goes on at eight thirty. See you tonight."

"See you." Sarah hung up the phone and shook her head. Great, now she had to find something to wear besides yoga pants and a T-shirt. Not to mention she should probably take a shower again.

There was something to be said for being a sloth who never left the house. Oh well.

BEFORE SHE'D EVEN stepped into the pub, she could hear the quick, giddy notes of a fiddle and a beautiful melodic male voice singing along to the upbeat song.

Sarah pushed open the doors to the pub and strode inside. Her footsteps faltered at the scene before her.

This was nothing like it had been during the afternoon where only a handful of customers had lingered. The McLaughlin Pub house was apparently the place to be at night. It was packed to the point of standing room only, and the dance floor was crowded with people actually dancing.

Glancing to the bar, she hoped to find a free stool, but it was equally packed. The crowd around the bar was three deep, waiting to get in their orders.

She spotted a blonde female bartender making drinks beside Aleck, but Kenzie was nowhere to be seen.

Overwhelmed by the crowd and growing more self-conscious by the moment, Sarah glanced back at the door and debated fleeing back to Gran's house.

"Sarah!" Someone caught her elbow, and she vaguely heard her name above the music.

She glanced up to find Colin grinning down at her.

"Come join us for a drink, luv." He gestured to a table in the corner. "I've got plenty of room."

"Great, thanks." She followed him back to the table and noted only one beer sitting there.

"Who else is here?" she asked, shrugging off her cardigan sweater. The crowd made it hot in here.

"Kenzie's working the floor, and Aleck is behind the counter." He paused. "Are you wondering if Ian is joining us?"

Her cheeks flushed and she gave a slight shrug.

"I don't right know, but there's always a chance." Colin's expression turned gentle. "Will you be okay if he does?"

"I'll be fine." Probably. Maybe.

"Aye, you will." He winked and waved down someone behind her. "What can I get you to drink?"

She glanced over her shoulder and saw Kenzie weaving her way through the crowd.

"Oh, um, maybe a glass of red wine?"

"Done. Kenzie, luv, get your friend a glass of—"

"I know what she likes." Kenzie leaned down to hug Sarah. "So good to see you here. Are you hungry?"

"I ate a little something earlier, thanks though."

Kenzie glanced at Colin. "Another beer, dear brother?"

"Not quite yet. Thanks, though."

With a nod, Kenzie disappeared into the crowd again.

Sarah turned her attention to the small stage near the back of the pub.

"'Whiskey in the Jar'?" She lifted a brow. "Isn't this an Irish song?"

"Aye, well I suppose it is," Colin agreed. "But it's a song about whiskey, so we don't hesitate to play it."

"And you shouldn't. It's a fantastic song. Do you sing too?"

He grinned. "Only when I've had too much to drink, and even then, not all that well. Kenzie and Aleck are the only two who you'll find on stage."

"I see. I'm pretty awful myself."

"I find that hard to believe. Pretty girls can't have awful singing voices. There's some kind of universal rule, I believe."

She laughed, unable to help herself, and tried to ignore the fact that Colin was bordering on flirting now. The McLaughlins flirted. Every last one of them, and they did it well.

"That's not a rule, and you would know it if you watched more music videos. Half these pop stars have zero talent."

"Aye, I suppose you're right. Can't stand music videos. I'm surprised you do."

"I don't actually. My daughter does." The laughter fled her voice and she knotted her fingers on the tabletop.

Awareness flickered in Colin's eyes and he nodded. "That's right, you have a child. Do you enjoy motherhood?"

"I do, but then, it's been my world for a while now."

"How long, you say?"

"Umm, almost nine years." Uncomfortable at the turn of conversation, and aware of the land mines she'd have to navigate, Sarah cleared her throat. "And you? Any children?"

"No. None of us have settled down and started families. Though I suppose we're all getting up in the age where we ought to consider it." Colin frowned. "Though Aleck came close. Was engaged for a bit, before that was called off."

"I find it amazing you're all still single. I'm sure you're all hot commodities on the island."

"Me in particular? Are you hitting on me?" His tone lilted upward, his accent a bit stronger as his grin turned unabashed.

Sarah blushed, hotter than she could remember and sputtered for a response. "No, of course not, I'm—"

"I'm just taking the piss out of ya, luv."

She relaxed and joined in his laughter, remembering the slang phrase now.

"I was asked to deliver this?"

They both glanced up at the new voice approaching the table.

Sarah's laughter died and her mouth went dry. *You were warned he might show.*

"Yes, thank you." She accepted the glass of wine from Ian and watched as he pulled out the chair to sit next to Colin.

"You're welcome. Enjoying an evening out I see?"

"I am. Kenzie invited me." She glanced over at Colin and smiled briefly. "Your brother was sweet enough to let me crash his table. This place was packed."

"I insisted." Colin winked.

The mood at the table seemed to shift, become heavier and darker. Seconds ticked by where no one said anything.

Sarah took a sip of wine, but really it may as well have been water for all it mattered.

"I'm going to run to the bathroom. Hold my spot?" She knew they would, but it was just extra words to pretend everything was normal.

"Of course," Colin agreed.

Sarah scooted her chair back and made her escape, grateful for a moment to compose herself.

∽

IAN WATCHED SARAH nearly run to the bathroom. Her hips swished beneath the denim skirt.

She looked sexy. The denim skirt showed off toned legs, and the red tank clung to the curves of her breasts. She'd kept her hair down, and it shone as if she'd spent an hour brushing it.

Oh yes, Sarah was trying tonight to look good. Almost as if she wanted to garner someone's attention. But who was that someone?

"You and Sarah seem quite cozy," he remarked in a calm tone he wasn't so sure he felt.

"Just getting reacquainted. She's a pretty thing, aye?"

"Aye." The word about killed him. Hearing his brother say it evoked a dark fury deep inside him. He resented it. Resented more so the fact he could still get jealous over Sarah.

"Why not take her to a movie?" he suggested with a hard shrug. "You're single."

Colin laughed and shook his head, before lifting the beer to his mouth and drinking another sip.

Unfortunately, his brother's reaction only upped his irritation. "You laugh? Why?"

"Because you don't mean that for a moment. You would saw my head off with a dull spoon if I made a move on Sarah."

"Bollocks." Actually, yes, he probably would.

"It's also a respect thing. Sarah's sweet, and yes, damn pretty." Colin sobered, his gaze locking on Ian's. "If she were just some girl you'd dallied with in high school, and had no real feelings for, then that would be one thing. But I'm not going to move in on a girl you're still half in love with."

Fury and disbelief erupted inside him. "Like hell—"

"Don't 'like hell' me. You can lie all you want. And, truly, I think you've even convinced yourself she means nothing to you. But you're wrong." Colin sighed. "And when you realize that, it's going to be quite a wake-up call."

"Do you have no recollection of our history? She hates me. I admit I hate her a bit after what she said that day—"

"Don't let pride stand in your way. You both were stupid and made bad choices that day."

"Mine a little worse," he muttered after a heavy sigh. "She won't forgive me. I hardly forgive myself."

"But if she did, would you want her back?"

That question weighed heavy on his heart, and he wasn't sure of the answer. How could he ever want to be with someone who thought so little of him? And yet his heart and body seemed to argue otherwise anytime she came within a few feet of him.

He settled for an answer his brother would expect. "I might want her for a few nights, but I'm not the sort for permanence."

Colin grunted. "You would with the right girl. Go ahead and throw crude words my way all you want. But I know you better than you know yourself sometimes."

Sometimes Ian didn't doubt it.

He played with the idea in his head. Could he ever be serious about Sarah again? Could he even gain her trust once more?

Do you deserve her trust? The question had always haunted him.

Their history was messy. Complicated. He'd be smarter off just letting go. So much easier said than done, though.

"I see I've at least got you thinking. That there is a novelty."

"Fuck off," Ian murmured lightly, knowing his brother

was just taking the piss out of him.

"Aye, maybe later. If I find someone who sparks the urge." Colin's gaze slid beyond him. "But your girl is coming back. You should pull yourself together a bit."

Your girl. As irritating as hearing it was, he did feel a bit territorial over Sarah. And apparently was acting it as well.

Shite. He'd have to be more careful.

He couldn't help but watch when she sat down. Her focus was on the band, while she took occasional sips of wine. But she had to sense he watched her—there was a stillness to her body, even as her gaze seemed deliberately glued to the stage.

Her lips tightened at one point, the plump curves almost pouting with unhappiness. And then those little lines appeared between her eyes in a tiny scowl.

Oh yeah. She was aware of him.

It just fascinated him. Made him want to get deeper into her head. Was she thinking about him? Thinking about that moment in the garage?

His fingers curled into fists and he drew in a slow, steadying breath.

She was so damn unattainable. Like a rare, exotically beautiful butterfly one could observe, but shouldn't touch.

And he wanted to touch. Wanted to taste. The need to possess her raged through him again. Just as fierce as it had the other day in his garage.

The band began to play an upbeat song and half the

ONE MORE ROUND

crowd got up to dance again. When a flicker of wistfulness entered her gaze it was all he needed.

"Come." He set down his drink and caught her hand. "You'll have to join me for a dance."

Panic replaced the wistfulness, and she tugged at her hand. "I can't—"

"Say yes. It's just a dance, doll." He tugged her onto the floor to join the crowd of people.

It wasn't a slow song, but a fast-moving one that had people hopping around in a somewhat chaotic jig fashion.

Though hesitant at first, it didn't take long before Sarah joined in. She kept space between them, but clearly enjoyed the enthusiasm of the crowd. Seemed to relax enough in his presence to have fun.

With her body moving to the beat, and her hair swinging wild, he had to fight the temptation to wrap the silky black strands around his fist and pull her closer. To press his mouth to the delighted smile on her lips.

Her cheeks were pink by the time the song ended and her smile was wide.

"Thank you. That wasn't bad exercise."

"My pleasure." And it had been. It wasn't enough, though. It would never be enough until she was lying beneath him and he was claiming her once more.

They rejoined Colin at the table and discovered Kenzie there as well.

Ian could feel the curious gazes of his siblings on him

and Sarah—knew what they were thinking—but he refused to acknowledge them.

"When do you sing, Kenzie?" he asked instead.

"I'm up next song. Care to join me?"

"Not at all. I have no wish to burst eardrums."

Everyone laughed, seeming to appreciate the humor.

Aleck approached the table, increasing the crowd of McLaughlins.

"Ian. Sarah. I must say it's great to see you both getting along so well."

Really? Ian was tempted to smash his beer bottle over Aleck's head, but instead just kept a lazy smile on his face.

"Well, now, it seemed the adult thing to do," Ian murmured.

"Aye. It is." Kenzie stood. "Time to sing. Try not to fall asleep on me now, all right?"

"As if I could. I can't wait to hear this." Sarah turned her chair a bit more and faced the stage.

Watching her, Ian could see she truly enjoyed hearing Kenzie sing, even clapped along with the melody as the tempo grew fast again. There was no denying Kenzie had the musical talent in the family.

The evening progressed, and his siblings came and went from the table, but he and Sarah stayed put for the most part. There was no more dancing, no intimate discussions, but they were deeply aware of each other. There was no denying he was, and he could still sense the tension running through her body.

Finally, with the night growing later, she stood. "I should probably head out."

When she dug into her purse for money, he waved her hand away.

"I've got you."

Alarm flashed in her eyes. Maybe he'd chosen the wrong words.

"It's a glass of wine. I insist."

"Besides," Aleck added as he passed the table again to pick up empty glasses from another one. "Haven't you realized your money is no good here?"

Her eyes widened with disbelief. "You guys…"

"Look, if you ran up a hundred-dollar tab, I might have to come down on you and charge half." Aleck shrugged. "But I'm afraid arguing at this point is useless."

Her cheeks reddened and she looked uncertain. "Okay," she finally relented. "But take my tip money."

She dropped a twenty on the table and rushed toward the door before anyone could argue.

"The cheeky lass." Colin grinned and reached for the money. "Don't mind if I do."

"Actually, I mind." Ian stood and plucked the bill from his brother and handed it to Kenzie. "You should be ashamed, stealing from your sister. She earned this."

"Appalling manners. The lot of you." Kenzie tucked the twenty into her bra. "And are none of you going to offer to drive her home?"

"Actually, I was making my way to do just that." Ian flashed a quick smile and strode toward the door.

Kenzie intercepted him before he reached it. "I'm glad you're driving her home, but don't mess things up this time."

"How would I mess things up?"

"Don't break her heart. It took her grandmother dying to return to the island. I've missed my best friend, and if you do anything—"

"I'll not do anything she doesn't want me to do," he said softly. "I love you, dear sister, but this really is none of your business."

She shook her head and fire flashed in her eyes. "I think it is, but I'll trust you. You're a good man, Ian. When you want to be."

"When I want to be," he agreed lightly, and then hurried outside after Sarah.

Chapter Ten

IAN SPOTTED HER when she was halfway across the gravel parking lot of the pub. She seemed to make her way to the street.

"Sarah," he called out. "Hold up, please."

She glanced over her shoulder, and he smiled when he heard her sigh of frustration.

"How are you getting home?"

"I took the bus, if you must know."

He caught up to her. "Let me drive you home."

"It'd really be better if you didn't."

"Might not be better, but it's safer. It's late. You shouldn't be out walking alone at night."

"The island isn't really all that dangerous from what I remember. Just the occasional deer bent on a suicide mission."

His lips twitched at that comment. "We may be safer than Seattle, but the island is not without crime."

And when you were a woman barely five feet tall, beautiful and out alone at night, you could be seen as an open invitation for an attack.

He didn't add that last bit, but knew she had the sense to have realized it. Though she had walked out of the bar alone, without even asking anyone to walk her to the bus stop.

Irritation pricked that she could be so foolish.

She was probably just trying to escape from you, his conscience argued. Still it did little to alleviate his irritation that she took her safety so lightly.

"I'd really rather take the bus—"

"And *I'm* really not negotiating with you on this, Sarah. Either you let me drive you home, or I'll toss you over my shoulder and place you in my car."

"Did you really just threaten to abduct me?" she sputtered.

Tired of her stalling, he took another step toward her. "*Sarah.*"

"Fine. I'll let you drive me home. But you can be such a bully," she grumbled, not looking pleased in the slightest.

"You call it bullying. I call it being protective." He gestured for her to walk in front of him. "I'm parked in the back."

Once they were in his car and heading to her gran's place, he made little effort to talk. Knew she wasn't really in the mood after he'd pretty much strong-armed her into getting in the car with him.

When he pulled up outside her house she'd opened the door before he'd even stopped.

"Thanks for the ride." She climbed out, slammed the door and ran toward the front porch.

Did she really think he'd let her scamper off that easily? He smothered a laugh and followed her.

✑

HEARING THE CAR door open, and then the sound of footsteps, Sarah's heart started pounding twice as fast.

Nighttime. A glass of wine. And that dance with Ian at the pub. It all equaled her having foolish thoughts she shouldn't be harboring.

"I don't need front-door service," she said tightly.

"It's included with the ride home." He stood beside her as she fumbled in her purse for her keys.

He wasn't making a move to touch her, and she said thanks silently for that. Because she knew the minute he did, she would come undone. It would be as if someone tugged the center of a bow that had already come loose.

She found her keys and then unlocked the door. Still, he didn't move.

"Thank you. And as you can see, I'm safely home." She stepped inside, the doorframe in a death grip between her fingers.

"Yes. I can see." He didn't move.

All she had to do was say goodnight and shut the door. That was it. She didn't move.

"Sarah."

Her name on his lips was almost a sigh of regret. A whisper for permission.

She didn't know what to say. To do. Emotion thickened in her throat and she struggled to breathe in. Her chest rose with the effort, and then shuddered as she exhaled raggedly.

He finally moved. Took the step to close the distance between them.

"Invite me in." His deep, honeyed words made everything inside her turn to liquid.

"What are you, a vampire?" she whispered, trying for humor. Anything to defuse the thick awareness and tension between them.

Their mutual need was so vibrant it was almost visible.

"No." He cupped her cheek. "I'm the man who's going to make you come at least five times tonight. If you'll let me."

Her panties dampened and her knees gave out. There was a moment she literally had to pull herself up and get a grip on herself.

His words didn't even shock her anymore. This was Ian. He lived to shock. Lived to offend. Nothing had changed.

Only he was even worse now. This man was trouble. He was a damn felon, for God's sake. Why was she even considering letting him into her life again? Let alone her body.

He wouldn't be good for her, and certainly not for Emily. Her heart twisted at that last thought and she shook her head.

"How long has it been since you've been touched?" His lips hovered over hers. "Since you've been with a man?"

Too long. Especially since her last experience was one she'd tried to block out.

"We can't do this."

"We can do whatever we please, doll. It's the beauty of being an adult. It doesn't have to be serious. It can simply be about the pleasure. About having fun while you're here." He brushed his lips across hers, so very lightly. "Are you looking for something more serious right now?"

"No." The idea of another relationship with him just distressed her. Made her stomach hurt. "But I don't know if I can do a fling."

"You could try. We're good together. You can't deny it."

They were. And that memory, combined with the way her body came to life with him now, was tempting her beyond the threshold of restraint.

He caught a strand of her hair and coiled it around a long finger. "You're more than a mother, Sarah. You deserve to feel like a woman for a bit. Let me help you."

It had been so long. And his words were too close to the thoughts she'd had that day in his garage.

Sex. Rarely did she have the urge for it. But since she'd come across Ian, the urges had not only been there, they'd been constant.

"You want to. It's something your body can't hide from me. Nor your eyes."

He kissed her then. His lips were firm, seeking, and pulling a reluctant response from her.

"I don't know if I can," she whispered when he lifted his head. "You're right. I want to..."

"I know I've hurt you." He kissed her forehead. "And I'm sorry. I'm going to try like hell not to do it again."

The sex would be good with him. So good. But could she do it? Just have great sex with Ian and walk away at the end of the month? Never look back?

No. Logic told her this was a bad, horribly bad, idea. But her body and heart were begging for more. Craved the intimate contact from the only man who'd ever truly brought her soul to life.

"Invite me inside," he urged again. "Let's see what happens. If you want me to stop—at any time—I swear to you I will."

She closed her eyes and drew in a slow breath. Then, ignoring the voice in her head that told her she'd regret it, she stepped back into the house and pushed the door open wide.

In the porch light she saw the flare of his nostrils and the darkening of his gaze. He didn't hesitate, but stepped into the house and closed the door behind them.

The loud grandfather clock in the living room ticked away, seeming like minutes passed, when it must've only been seconds.

He again took control—which she was thankful for, because she didn't know what the hell to do next—pulling her fully into his arms.

Her body pressed flush against his. He was so hard and unyielding, while her breasts crushed against his chest to accommodate.

His mouth took hers again, but it wasn't a gentle or light kiss. It was deep and demanding. A warning that the road ahead could be pretty damn intense.

It thrilled her.

She kissed him back, throwing all her hesitations to the wind. She must have subconsciously known that the moment she'd stepped foot on this island, and realized they were both single, this moment was inevitable.

Every nerve end on her body was aflame. She needed him to touch her. Everywhere. A whimper of need passed her lips as she pressed herself harder against him, stroking her tongue over his.

He slid a hand between them, cupping her breast through her tank top, and she moaned low in her throat as a tremble wracked through her.

It wasn't enough.

She tore her mouth from his and whispered a ragged, "Please. I need more."

Before he could make a move, she stepped back to pull off her top, unable to meet his gaze though.

"So pretty."

She flushed when he murmured the soft words. She knew her bra and underwear weren't sexy, just plain white cotton that did the job. But she was a single working mom who had little time for dating—let alone sex.

If she'd let herself consider the possibility of *this* happening then she might've gone shopping before flying out here. Oh, who was she kidding? If she'd suspected this was a possibility she would've just given up on inheriting Gran's house.

"Don't look so skeptical." He laughed softly. "You're beautiful."

"I'm plain."

He shook his head and the heat in his eyes made her dampen further.

"You are nowhere near plain. Why don't I show you exactly what you do to me?"

Her mouth went dry as he unhooked the back clasp of her bra and tossed it to the ground.

His groan of appreciation sent chills of anticipation through her. Then his hands replaced the bra, cupping her and teasing her nipples to stiff peaks.

Pleasure spiked through her and she pressed into him, her breathing already turning ragged.

He abandoned her breasts and she gave a murmur of protest, which died when he grabbed her ass and lifted her. She wrapped her legs around his waist, holding on as he crossed the floor to the sofa.

After dropping her onto the cushions, his body soon followed. The weight of him pressed her down as he slid a knee between her legs.

Her denim skirt hiked up, which he only encouraged by grabbing the ends and tugging it above her hips.

His head dipped, nuzzling her breasts. He'd just flicked his tongue over one tip when she felt the brush of his fingers over her panties.

"Mmm." His throat rumbled against her chest. "You're already soaking wet for me."

She didn't even have time to be self-conscious about the statement, because then he drew her nipple into his mouth and began to suck.

Pleasure built rapidly inside of her. Spiraling so dangerously high she knew she'd fall hard.

He didn't remove her panties, just found and teased her hot spot through the fabric.

Gripping his shoulders, she breathed heavier, not bothering to smother her cries of pleasure. Her hips lifted against his touch and her toes curled as she got closer to a climax.

When he grazed his teeth over her nipple she was pushed over the edge.

OH HELL BUT he'd missed this. Missed her.

Ian watched as Sarah rode out her orgasm. She'd locked her legs around his hand, but he didn't stop rubbing her clit through the damp, soft fabric.

When her lashes finally fluttered open, the blue of her

eyes was shiny with passion and her lips were parted.

That mouth. He turned his attention to her lips. He hardened at the idea of sliding his cock past them and deep into her mouth.

Would she still take him that way? Damn, but he wanted to find out.

But first, there was so much else he wanted. Like to see her completely unclothed.

He couldn't resist leaning down to take one dark red nipple into his mouth again.

She whimpered, squirming beneath his body.

"Take off your clothes." She lifted her hips as she made the plea. "Please, I want to feel you against me."

"Give me a moment, doll." A strained smile pulled at his mouth. "There's so much I want to do to you first."

Like tear those damn panties from her body and bury his face between her legs. He needed to see if she still tasted as sweet as he remembered.

"Lift your hips again," he commanded softly.

When she did, he caught her skirt and pulled it off her. Then went back to grab the edge of her cotton panties, tugging them off her thighs and down her legs.

The sight he unveiled had his mouth drying out.

"You're killing me here." He tossed the panties to the side and then went back to discover everything he'd been missing for eleven years.

Her curves were more emphasized now. Sexier. Her

breasts larger and the nipples darker. Her stomach was still just as flat, but decorated with a few silvery lines as a badge of motherhood. And lower on her abdomen, a tiny horizontal scar that hinted her daughter had been born via C-section.

He slid his gaze lower. To the trimmed black curls just above a smooth mound that already shimmered with her arousal. He touched her lightly there, spreading the folds and easing a finger inside her.

She whimpered softly and her body clenched around his finger. She was hot and wet. Her sheath gripped his finger the deeper he went.

Soon it wouldn't be his finger, but his cock, and the realization had him rock hard.

With his free hand he reached down to unfasten his jeans to give himself a bit more room to breathe.

"Ian," she whispered. "Oh, please. Don't stop."

He added a second finger, stretching her and testing her readiness. He'd wanted to taste her. To bring her to orgasm at least one more time before taking her. But he knew he wouldn't last. Not with the way she was panting and riding his hand.

It wasn't enough.

While still warming her up with his fingers, he freed himself completely from his jeans. Her eyes were closed and her breathing erratic.

He needed her. Now.

Pushing her thighs wider, he pulled his hand away from her and replaced it with his cock. Thrusting home.

Sarah cried out as her eyes snapped open, rounding with shock and pleasure.

"Sorry, doll. I couldn't wait."

"I didn't want you to." Her husky words sent a shudder of pleasure through him.

He held her gaze as he sank deeper. Damn, she was tight. The times before he'd sworn he was too big for her, with her being so petite, but she'd always promised he wasn't.

And even now, when he started to worry, her body hugged him with slick warmth, encouraging him forward. So did the small gasps of pleasure she made.

She slid her hands up his chest, grasping his shoulders as he began to move inside her.

Vaguely he realized that while she was stark naked, he hadn't even taken off his clothes.

"Take me," she whispered, wrapping her legs around his hips. "Please, Ian, don't hold back."

He wanted it hard this time, and she'd just given him the go-ahead.

Abandoning all hesitation, he plunged into her with the urge his body demanded.

Blindly, he sought her clit again with a finger, rubbing it as he rode her harder and faster.

When her body tightened and she was about to come, he responded. He was nearly there. Felt the whiteness of orgasm take over his mind, when he realized why it was so good.

Forgot the condom.

With a groan, he pulled out at the last moment and spilled himself on her stomach.

Sarah didn't seem too bothered as she trembled through her own release, her soft cries their soundtrack in the silent house.

"Sorry," he murmured after a minute or two. "I didn't plan that."

He nuzzled her breast, placing a kiss on one hard tip. The sound of her heartbeat was still a frantic thump.

"We spaced on protection," she agreed.

"Yeah."

She reached up to push a strand of hair off his forehead. "Thank you for, um, doing what you did."

He laughed softly. She was thanking him for that? Some girls would probably have preferred to punch him.

"Let me grab you a washcloth." He eased off her and crossed the living room toward the bathroom. Thankfully the front curtains were shut, or he'd be giving the houses scattered below her quite the show.

After cleaning himself up in the bathroom, he returned with a warm, damp washcloth.

She hadn't moved from the couch, but instead had her arms thrown above her head now as she stared at the ceiling.

He settled on the edge of the couch and ran the cloth over her stomach.

"Are you all right?" he asked, when she still didn't say anything.

"I'm fine." She gave a slight nod. "Just…thinking."

About what had just happened between them no doubt. Did she regret it?

"I never forget a condom. I blame you. You go to my head."

"Actually, it wouldn't be the first time you forgot a condom."

"Yes, it is."

She stared at him. "No. It isn't."

Shite, what wasn't he remembering? Ian scavenged his memory, trying to remember. Something pricked at the shadows of his mind.

Her expression turned skeptical. "Wait, you really don't remember?"

"I'm trying to."

"Never mind." She shook her head and scooted into sitting position. "It was a long time ago and totally irrelevant."

It clicked. "The morning after prom, right?"

"Right." She crossed the room, heading straight to the bathroom now.

He followed her. "We woke up, went at it, and then realized we'd forgot."

"Bingo. See there? Not always so on the protection ball."

"Yes, well you're the only one. And really, twice in fifteen years isn't all that bad of a record."

"Fifteen years?" She paused at the bathroom door and turned to look at him. "You lost your virginity at fourteen?"

"Aye." He grinned. "A going away from Scotland present from my neighbor, Mrs. Robinson."

Sarah snorted. "How original. I suppose she was an older woman?"

"How'd you know?"

"Lucky guess."

"She was divorced. Quite lovely and with jugs—"

"Don't need to hear it. Thanks." She waved a hand in his face and disappeared into the bathroom.

"Are you showering?"

"Yes." She paused and pulled the door open enough to stick her head out again. Her eyes were narrowed, but there was amusement in them. "Did you want to join me?"

Aye. Hell yeah, he did. "Thought you'd never ask, doll."

He slipped into the bathroom with her, already semi-hard again at the thought of taking her in the shower.

One thing was certain. If Sarah had any regrets about tonight, she had a funny way of showing it.

Chapter Eleven

FIVE DAYS. SHE'D lasted five days on the island before falling back into bed with Ian McLaughlin.

Sarah lay still in bed, staring at the ceiling and the hint of daylight that trickled in through the blinds.

Beside her Ian still slept, his soft snores not bothering her in the least. Now, his blatant nudity and the leg thrown across hers was another story.

Why hadn't she thrown on a T-shirt before falling asleep? Some type of article of clothing that would put a barrier between them. It was a potent reminder of what had happened. Twice last night.

But did she regret it? The question had looped in her head as she'd fallen asleep, and then again when she'd opened her eyes.

The answer wasn't quite clear. She'd enjoyed the sex too much to regret it. But the underlying fear of what she was risking put a damper on what had happened.

And what if it were about more than just sex? The idea had flitted through her head more than once, but she refused to dwell on the possibility too long. It couldn't be more.

She tried to roll to her side a little so she could look at him.

He was so close to her, his body turned toward hers. In his sleep Ian appeared completely at peace. His brows, which were often drawn together in a scowl, were completely relaxed. His lips were parted as he breathed slow and steadily.

As if sensing her perusal, or maybe her movement, he reached out for her. Of course his hand landed on a breast and her breath caught on a choked gasp.

For a moment he stayed asleep, his hand just resting there. But she knew the moment he woke up enough to realize what he was grasping.

His fingers, initially immobile, began to trace her flesh. To cup her breast, and then knead.

She closed her eyes tightly and bit her lip. They weren't going to go another round, were they? Surely he was burnt out by now. She was.

He caught her nipple between his fingers and pinched slightly. While the tip tightened under his touch, warmth flooded her body and moisture gathered between her legs.

Oh well, she'd thought she was burnt out.

"Still a morning person, huh?" he murmured and gave a low, raspy laugh that just screamed sleepy male and sex.

"Most of the time." Oh why did her voice have to crack? Did she have to sound all breathy?

He squeezed her breast again and then leaned over to place a kiss on the nipple.

Her lashes fluttered up and she found his gaze on her face.

"Hi." He leaned down to kiss her lips.

When he lifted his head, she repeated a soft, "Hi."

The hand that held her breast slid downward, tracing circles over her stomach. Already butterflies were having a rave inside there, but when he traced his fingers even lower, she couldn't stop a low moan.

"Sarah." Her name was almost a sigh on his lips. His gaze darkened and searched hers. "Last night was…"

Amazing? A mistake? She wished he'd finish the thought, because she was still in the undecided category herself.

But he didn't finish his words. Instead he moved his hand those last few inches and cupped the heated flesh between her legs.

He dipped a finger into her and she whimpered, unable to tear her gaze away from his.

"I can't wait to fuck you again."

Shock ripped through her arousal. For a moment she wondered if she'd heard him right, but then he parted her thighs and moved between them.

"Ian—"

"I know." He lowered himself onto her and kissed her, his tongue demanding a response as she felt the nudge of his erection into her sex.

Asshole. After everything that had happened last night, he was back to his crude, heartless self? Her brain screamed in fury, but her body wasn't getting the message. The two were at war, and she knew which one was losing.

Especially when she felt the thick length of him slide into her. All desire to push him away vanished, because it was just too good.

He broke the kiss and lifted his head, staring down at her.

She hated him. And yet, a part of her was terrified she still loved him. While she couldn't seem to bring herself to push him away physically, he made it easier to keep herself away emotionally.

Sarah closed her eyes, unable to meet the heat in his gaze anymore, and gripped his shoulders. Her nails nearly pierced the skin as her body adjusted to accommodate him.

It had always been like this. So much pleasure, even though sometimes it felt as if he were just too big. But Ian had always ensured she was ready for him. Her comfort and pleasure had been a priority. He could be an asshole in some ways, but in others he was wonderfully tender.

He was nothing like her ex-husband. Immediate nausea rose, and she had to push the thought of Neil aside. Focus instead on Ian and the pleasure of this moment.

He moved deeper into her, increasing the pace of his thrusts. Her hips rose to meet each stroke, and together they found their rhythm.

Her body built toward climax. Her breathing grew heavier and she couldn't stop her cries of pleasure. What would it matter if she did? He knew his effect on her. How her body would always be his, even if she guarded her heart so much better.

Always so in tune to her body, he reached between them and found her clit. One stroke and she was over the edge. And he followed right after her.

Still wracked by the remains of her climax, her mind kicked back into action.

He hadn't pulled out this time.

Pleasure was replaced by a thick, seizing panic. She pushed at his shoulders, trying to get out from under him.

"Sarah?" he frowned, confusion and passion clouding his gaze. "What's…ah, fuck. We forgot again."

She could see the realization kick in with him too, and yet he didn't move right away.

Shit. Oh God, shit.

"Calm down, Sarah." His voice gentled. "Are you on any kind of birth control?"

"No, of course not." She shook her head. The last person she'd been with had been her ex-husband. And that had been a couple of years ago.

"Really?" The first bit of unease flickered in his eyes. "Do you know where you are in your cycle?"

Drawing in a breath, she tried to slow her mind enough to think about that.

"I finished just before I came to Whidbey."

He eased off her. "You're probably going to be okay."

"What are you, a freaking obstetrician?" She slid away from him, furious at herself. At him. "What was I thinking? It's not just the terrifying possibility of getting pregnant. You could have God knows what kind of STD."

He stared at her. Hard. There was a different kind of heat in his eyes now—one driven by anger instead of passion. She watched the small tic in his jaw.

"Well, that sure as hell didn't seem to bother you last night. I might've pulled out, but that doesn't always mean anything," he said tersely. "I'm clean. If you want me to get a new test to show you, I will. And I sure as hell don't want any kids, so you can be assured this isn't exactly sitting well with me either."

She placed her fingers on her temples and shook her head, feeling as if she wanted to throw up. Her heart screamed how much she hated him. And again, hated herself. Why had she brought him back into her life? Her body?

She was the queen of bad decisions. That would always be a given in her life. Especially when it came to him.

"Get out," she whispered.

"Sarah, look, there's no—"

"Get out, Ian." She should've said it fifteen minutes ago, but better late than never. Climbing off the bed, she strode to the bathroom. "I don't want to talk. I don't want to see you. I don't want you in my life anymore. Got it?"

There was no reply, and she turned at the door to the bathroom. He sat on the edge of the bed, watching her. His expression was unreadable.

"Yeah. I got it."

Then he slid out of bed and reached to grab the clothes on the ground. Her gaze unwittingly slid over the green Celtic knot tattoo that covered half his back and shoulder blades. She watched the muscles of his body ripple as he tugged on his clothes.

He truly had an extraordinary body. Was good in bed. And she was a sucker for it. That was the only way she could possibly rationalize what'd happened in the last twenty-four hours. Her complete lapse of sanity.

Whatever helps you sleep at night, her mind whispered, not buying the excuses.

"Well thanks for the fun, doll." His tone was flat. "Be sure to let me know if I knocked you up."

A hysterical laugh bubbled in her throat, but she swallowed it back down. Just like eleven years ago, her words had hit their mark and Ian was pissed.

Without a backward glance, Ian left the bedroom and a few minutes later she heard the front door click shut.

Tears blurred her eyes as she moved back into the bedroom to find her cell phone. It might be barely six here, but her mom was three hours ahead. Unfortunately it went straight to voicemail.

She left a message anyway. "I need to borrow some money, Mom. Maybe five hundred until I get paid again. I'm having Gran's car repaired. Call me back and let me know if you can afford it."

Once she disconnected the call, she curled up into a ball and let the tears fall. She must've fallen back asleep at some point, because her phone ringing woke her up. A quick glance at the caller ID showed it was her mom.

Sarah picked up with a groggy hello.

"Sorry I missed your call, Sarah. We're out and about. Sure I can lend you money." Her mom sounded distracted. "Are you all right? You sound...a little awful, actually."

"I'm just stressed." *And heartbroken.* "I really miss Em." That much wasn't a lie.

"I know. She misses you too. Hang on a second." There was a pause as her mother seemed to be speaking to someone else. "Okay, I'm back."

Tears fell silently down her cheeks. She tried to keep it together. "So you can send the money online?"

"I can mail you a check or something. I don't do that online thing. One second—" There was another muffled silence. "Look, I must run...I'll talk to you later, okay? I just didn't want you to think I was ignoring your call."

A little disappointed her mom was brushing her off, she said, "Sure. No problem."

"And pull yourself together, Sarah." Her mother's voice dropped an octave. "Whatever it is, it'll get better."

"I know." But what if it didn't? What if it got worse?

﹏

"BOSS, YOU GOT a—"

"I said no phone calls," Ian snarled when someone popped their head into his office.

"Ugh, yeah. Sorry about that. I forgot." Looking chagrined, and a little stunned, Carl backed out of the office at the garage and shut the door.

Fuck.

Ian thrust a hand through his hair and closed his eyes. He was in a shitty mood, no doubt about it. Anyone who came too close this morning was likely to get his head bitten off. It'd already happened a handful of times. Which made him wonder why people kept approaching him.

After leaving Sarah's this morning, he'd gone home to shower and change, and then showed up late to work.

Maybe he should've just called in sick. Because he sure as hell felt pretty crappy now.

Which was ironic, because he'd woken up happy as a clam.

Happy was pretty much an understatement. This morning he'd felt like the hero in some animated love story. It was all sunshine and roses. He could've been using the toilet and birds would've been singing a love song in the background.

Life was amazing. He'd woken up next to Sarah, and he'd been content. Almost relieved to have her back in his arms again. It had felt so right. As if Sarah were his destiny and always had been. They'd just taken a wrong turn down the road of their relationship.

When he'd woken and found himself touching her, he'd almost said *I want to make love to you again.* The words had been on the tip of his tongue. And then his mind had overridden all the nonsense his heart was trying to convince him of.

Their relationship never was and never would be a fairy tale. Sarah being back on the island was temporary. Maybe the sex between them was awesome, and he could make her orgasm with barely any effort, but the bottom line was she still didn't like him much. Maybe once they'd had that emotional connection, but now it was nothing more than a physical thing for them both.

So instead of the sappy love-filled words he'd wanted to say, he'd kept it crude. Had said he wanted to fuck her again, half-expecting her to push him away. To climb out of bed and tell him to go to hell.

But she hadn't. There'd been a flash of shock in her eyes, and maybe something deeper. Hurt? No, that would mean she gave two shits about him.

So he'd nudged her thighs apart and sank into her. He'd found her wet and ready for him. Her body eager to accept him, even as he could see her mind was probably trying to talk her out of it.

And he'd hated himself at that moment. So much. He'd just lost himself in her body. With her nails leaving tracks on his back, he'd completely lost his mind. He'd taken her until the only thing he could think of was claiming her completely again. Until she'd cried out his name and he'd emptied himself into her.

She'd had every right to freak out. While he hadn't lied about being STD-free, getting pregnant was obviously on her *Do Not Do* list. She was probably overwhelmed with Emily alone.

Hell, it wasn't like he wanted a kid either, did he?

Christ. He'd fucked up, but good.

The door to his office burst open and he lifted his head, ready with another snarl of rage.

It died on his tongue when he spotted Kenzie in the doorway, eyes blazing.

"*You're* not answering my calls. *Sarah's* not answering my calls." She slammed the door. "You'd better start talking, and now. What happened last night?"

Crap. His sister couldn't help but shove her nose in everyone else's business. Especially his and Sarah's. Though it shouldn't surprise him. She'd always been protective of him—more so in the last few years, and Sarah would always be her close friend.

It was only a given that Kenzie would try and get in the middle of his and Sarah's clusterfuck and try and fix things. But some things weren't fixable.

With his irritation completely erased at Kenzie's presence, wariness took its place.

"Look, Kenzie, I mean this in the most loving way, but

stay out of my damn business. I'd rather not have to say it again."

"Oh, Ian...I told you not to hurt her." Disappointment flickered in his sister's eyes as she sat on the edge of the desk.

And he had. But then she'd done a damn good job at hurting him right back, hadn't she?

"Whatever you did wrong, can you fix it?" she asked hopefully.

"I don't think so, kid. Not this time."

This morning had been eerily similar to that morning eleven years ago. Only without the bit where he'd been caught cheating.

Just running that thought through his head made him a little nauseous with self-disgust. How was it he still couldn't remember that night, and yet felt such shame?

Kenzie shook her head. "I don't get you two. You're clearly meant to be together—"

"No. Don't make this all romantic, Kenzie. If there's anything between us, it's good old-fashioned lust. Pure and simple."

His sister stared at him. "Why don't you think you're good enough for her?"

"Because I'm not." Christ. In a moment Kenzie had cut to the heart of the matter. To confront the reality he couldn't face.

"You are." Her words were soft, but strong. "Why do you think you're not? Because you're a felon?"

He didn't answer. Because again, she'd nailed a part of it.

"We both know that's bullshit."

"It's not bullshit, it's my reality."

Pain flashed in Kenzie's eyes. "If I could go back to that night—"

"I wouldn't change a thing."

"I would," she said huskily. "You can't let that label define you. You're an amazing man."

Not even close. An amazing arsehole, perhaps.

"Does Sarah know about…?"

"Yes."

"Did you tell her why?"

"It doesn't matter. Once Sarah leaves this island, she's gone from my life again." He didn't bother to soften his words. "And honestly it's better that way."

"Oh, *bullshit.*" Kenzie slapped his desk and got right in his face. "Ian, you can't bury your head in your job and spend your days fixing cars all the time. That's no kind of life." She jammed her finger into his chest. "And you need to stop sleeping with various bimbos in hopes they'll erase Sarah from your mind. No one is *ever* going to replace her."

Unfortunately he'd already come to that painful realization himself. Since she'd returned to the island, Sarah was all he'd thought about. All he'd ever wanted, and everything he would never have.

"You're still a romantic, dear sister." He stood and cupped her face, kissing the top of her forehead. "It's what I love about you. Don't ever change."

"I'm a realist. Even if you're both too blind to see the truth, someone has to." Kenzie slid off his desk and pulled her keys from the pocket of her jeans. "I'm off to drop by Sarah's house and make sure she's okay."

She wasn't. He knew it instinctively. He recalled the way she'd ordered him to leave. The way she'd emotionally shut down on him. And after the way he'd treated her, he'd deserved it.

Heaviness settled on his heart and regret became a bitter taste on his tongue.

Later tonight he'd drop by Sarah's and apologize. He wouldn't try to seduce her. Wouldn't invite himself in for a drink.

Perhaps he'd screwed up more times than he could count where Sarah was concerned, but there was one thing left he could do to make things right between them.

That was to finally let her go.

Chapter Twelve

NOT AGAIN.

Sarah sighed, reluctant to open the door to the insistent knock. But she did so anyway, and faced her guest.

"I'm not really good company right now, Kenzie."

"I gathered, seeing as you didn't answer my call. Or my texts." Kenzie stepped in through the doorway. "You know that's going to make me worry, right?"

"I'm sorry. Honestly, I'm not even sure where my phone is."

"Not a problem. I can simply help you find it."

Kenzie wasn't going to leave, but then she hadn't really expected her friend to go so easily.

"Don't you have to work at the pub or something?" Sarah closed the door and followed Kenzie into the house.

"Actually, I'm off today. Lucky for you." Kenzie crossed to the counter in the kitchen. "Oh, look. Here's your phone."

Crap.

"It's always in the most obvious place, isn't it?" Sarah

murmured with a slight shrug.

Kenzie shifted the phone from one hand to another, staring hard at Sarah.

"You look just as awful as he does."

Sarah's mouth fell open and she blinked in dismay. "Excuse me? I've showered—"

"Okay, props for not stinking. But you both look like you've gone through an emotional hurricane."

Sarah's chest tightened and she was thankful there were no more tears to cry.

"Oh, Kenzie… I know you mean well. But you've got to let it go."

"What's keeping you two from being together?"

"What's not?" Sarah hesitated. "There's just so much. We don't stand a chance."

"You guys have an amazing chemistry."

"Yes, well so do Mentos and diet soda, but they don't last forever. In the end you're just left with a complete mess."

Kenzie nodded slowly. "Is it what happened with him and Hailey back then? I'm not going to argue that he messed up, big time. I'll give you that."

"It's part of it," she agreed softly.

How could someone you loved, who claimed to love you more than anything, go and sleep with one of your best friends? How did you ever get past that?

"He was only eighteen. I know it doesn't excuse it, but he was probably like every other teenage guy thinking with his dick." Kenzie's face scrunched. "And from what I under-stand, Hailey came on to him. Which still shocks the hell out of me. I never expected her to play such a blatant slut card."

Ouch. She winced at the harsh words for the woman they'd once considered a close friend.

"Maybe it was the alcohol?" Sarah suggested, not sure why she was defending either of them. "But they both made the decision that night."

"It was so long ago." Kenzie hesitated. "If Ian means as much to you as I think he does, maybe you could try for-giveness?"

Would it ever be that easy? "Would you be able to if you were in my place?"

"I don't know, honestly." Kenzie hesitated, seeming to think on it. "But if I loved someone...or thought I did, I think I would truly try."

Sarah closed her eyes. If only it were that easy. If only things weren't such an absolute mess. Coming back to the island had been a mistake. She shouldn't have opened a door that had been sealed shut. It risked the life she'd gone on to build without Ian.

Bringing him back into it at this point... A chill swept through her and she shook her head.

"It can't work, Kenzie. Ian and I are too different."

Kenzie looked as if she wanted to say something, and then bit her lip. She shook her head instead.

"Maybe you're different, but you're also alike in more ways than you think. You need each other." She set Sarah's cell phone on the counter again and walked to the living room window. "Maybe I'm the only one who can see it, but I know the man my brother is beneath the badass exterior. Even if he's so determined to present that hard, intimidating side to the world."

Sarah didn't try to argue, because even though she knew Ian still had a dark side, he also had a good side. She'd seen it. She'd fallen in love with it. But it wasn't enough anymore. Even if she could forgive what had happened eleven years ago, she still had to think about Emily.

Ian was a felon, and apparently he still ran with the criminal sort. What kind of mom willingly exposed her child to that?

Again she thought of the man in his shop the other day, the one Ian had warned her to stay away from. Kenzie couldn't possibly know about the type of business her brother did or she wouldn't be so supportive of setting them up again.

But even if there wasn't the felony, there more. There was always more.

I sure as hell don't want any kids. His words from this morning rang sharp in her mind again. Had been resonating all day.

She'd made the right choice in not trying to stay eleven years ago. And she was making the right choice now. This wasn't about forgiveness; this was about common sense.

Maybe Ian was the type of guy you slept with, but you sure didn't keep him in your life. Unfortunately her heart was really bad at keeping that line drawn in the sand.

Sarah touched her friend's shoulder gently. "Look, this topic is kind of heavy. Why don't we go walk into town? Get an early dinner on the dock? It's gorgeous outside."

Kenzie stared out the window for a bit longer, seeming lost in her own thoughts. Almost unhappy.

Finally she turned and nodded. "Yeah, sure. That sounds good."

They left the house and made the short walk into the adorable town of Coupeville where most of the businesses were on Front Street, right along the water.

Fortunately, their conversation stayed away from Ian now, and on light and neutral topics. Like the fact that Kenzie was taking online classes to get her paralegal degree. That little fact was somewhat of a surprise to Sarah. She'd never realized her friend harbored any interest in the legal field whatsoever.

They turned onto the wharf and walked out onto the structure that was over a century old. The historical wharf with the red building at the end was a well-recognized landmark of the town. So beautiful, rustic and with a fascinating history.

She remembered the locals telling how once, before the Deception Pass Bridge had been built, there had been a steamboat service from Seattle to the Coupeville wharf that had brought people to the island.

Even now, as she walked out on the old wooden boards next to Kenzie, she could visualize what it must've been like a century ago. But then, she'd always been fascinated by history and old photographs.

She was so busy reacquainting herself with the view that it took a moment to realize Kenzie had gone silent.

"Kenz? You okay?"

"Shit." The word was almost a whisper, but it was thick with tension.

Following Kenzie's gaze, she spotted the group of men walking up the plank onto the wharf from a dock that moored a bunch of boats.

"What's going on? Who are they?"

Kenzie didn't reply, just shook her head. Her jaw clenched and Sarah could've sworn her friend was considering jumping off the side of the wharf to avoid the inevitable confrontation.

"Kenzie McLaughlin," one of the guys called out. He was tall and blond. Kind of preppy-looking, and altogether too pretty for Sarah's taste. "You're still looking damn fine, my little Highland Hottie."

The men he was with all snickered as they stared at Kenzie as if she were a prime cut of meat.

Jerkwads. All of them.

Sarah snuck another glance at Kenzie, wondering how

she'd react. Just waiting for her friend to rip them to bits. But she wasn't even looking at them as she increased her stride to pass them.

"Where you going, baby? Why don't you come hang out on my boat for a few and we can have some fun?"

Their ensuing laughter irked Sarah, and she was tempted to spout off something she shouldn't, but she bit her tongue. Fortunately the men kept walking.

At the end of the wharf, Kenzie nearly ran inside the building.

Sarah caught up to her. "Hey, are you okay?"

"Fine. Just craving coffee and food."

"Umm. You're not even going to tell me who those idiots were?"

"Well, you nailed it. They're idiots." Kenzie's smile was hard though. "Let's get a table okay? I need to eat."

There was a story there, but obviously Kenzie wasn't about to get into it. Not now anyway. Sarah tucked away that little tidbit of info.

"Sure." She nodded slowly and gave her friend a reassuring smile. "I'm actually pretty hungry myself."

⌢

AFTER WORK IAN walked from his shop to Sarah's house since it was only a few minutes away.

But when he spotted Kenzie's car in the driveway, he hesitated.

Hell. He didn't really want an audience for this whole apology scenario he had in his head. But then again, maybe it would help to have her there. She could be a defuser to the situation. Ensure he wouldn't try to jump Sarah's bones again, because that would just be awkward with his sister watching.

After knocking on the front door a few times and getting no response, Ian dug his cell from his pocket and sent his sister a text to find out where they were.

She replied back a moment later saying they'd walked into town to have dinner out on the wharf. And why did he want to know where she was anyway?

He gave a slight smile and shook his head. Shite. Maybe the apology would have to wait.

Shoving his phone back into his pocket, he turned to walk back down the porch steps. The car that turned into the driveway slowed him down. Looked like a rental. It came to a stop a few feet away.

With the sun behind the car, it wasn't easy to make out the driver, but she emerged a minute later.

Eleven years had passed, and Ana Thornton had barely aged. Maybe a few more wrinkles and some gray hairs in her short bob, but Sarah's mother could almost pass as her older sister.

Uncertain of how she'd react to seeing him, he hesitated on the porch, thrusting his hands into the back pockets of his jeans.

"Ian McLaughlin." She took a cautious step forward. "Is that you? Or am I confusing you with Colin?"

"You had it right the first time." A faint smile tugged at his lips and beneath his discomfort there was a familiar fondness for Sarah's mom. "You look well, Ana."

"And you're a good liar, but thank you. I'm sure I look about as awful as I feel after traveling all day, I guess." She grimaced and glanced past him toward the house.

"Has your husband come with you?" he asked mildly, trying not to let his expression turn bitter with the words.

The idea of seeing Sarah's dad made his gut clench, but he'd face the man if needed. He'd never been one to walk away from a confrontation.

"No." Her lashes fluttered down. "Ed died from a heart attack three years ago."

Now he struggled to hide his shock. Ed had passed away? Sarah had never mentioned it since her return.

"I'm sorry," he murmured a bit lamely.

"Thank you." She gave a brief smile and glanced up again, looking past him. "Are you…spending time with Sarah?"

"No. Well, aye. A bit." He paused. "I didn't realize you were coming out."

Guilt flickered in Ana's eyes before she cleared her throat. "No. Neither does Sarah."

Really? Sarah had no idea her mother was coming to Whidbey? Now that was going to be a shock and a half.

The sound of another car door opening had his attention shifting beyond Ana.

He stilled at the sight of the small girl exiting the vehicle. Sarah's daughter. No doubt about it.

"Emily, I asked you to wait in the car."

The little girl shrugged, her pretty face—so much like her mother's—crinkled into a scowl.

"I was bored in there. And I feel sick, Grandma. We've been driving for too long."

She was Sarah's mini-me. Her hair wasn't quiet as dark as Sarah's, maybe a little more brown than black, but it was long and shiny just like her mother's. She was adorable and delicate in her denim shorts and a pink glittery tank top with matching sparkly pink sunglasses.

"We drove here straight from Sea-Tac," Ana explained. "Before that we had about five hours on a plane."

"Understandable. That's a long time to travel."

Shite this was a trip. Sarah's daughter was here, standing right in front of him. Staring up at him with blatant curiosity, her hands on her hips.

"Where's my mom?"

"Umm, she's gone for a walk."

"I don't understand why people walk for fun. Who are you?"

And here came the questions.

"Ian."

"I'm Emily. Sarah's my mom."

"So I gathered."

"Are you friends with her?" She continued, barely taking a breath. "Did you know she's single now? She can date."

Christ. How old was this little matchmaker again? He could feel the heat in his neck as he struggled to answer that question. Children were just filterless little explosives, weren't they?

"Emily, don't be rude."

Even while grateful for Ana's intervention, Ian still couldn't help but be amused by Emily.

"I'm not rude, Grandma. I was just telling him." Emily rolled her eyes, before glancing curiously at the house. "Was this my great-grandma's house?"

"Yes," Ian answered before Ana could.

Emily's attention slid to the yard that circled the entire house. "Grandma, is that grass part of the house?"

"Yes."

"Woo whoo!"

Ian watched as she kicked off her flip-flops and sprinted toward the stretch of grass that was the widest.

"Emily." Ana sighed and shook her head, but it was the only effort she made to stop her granddaughter as she launched into a handspring.

Just like her mama.

Somewhat alarmed that she was going to break something, Ian clenched his hands into fists and held his breath until Emily landed safely on her feet.

"She nearly gives me a heart attack every time she does that," Ana muttered. "She's just like her mother was. Gymnastics is in her blood."

He watched as Emily grabbed her sunglasses, which had fallen off, from the ground and slid them back on.

"I remember Sarah loved it as well. Emily's quite good for being so young, aye?"

"I suppose." Ana gave him a considering, sidelong glance. "So Sarah's gone on a walk?"

"She and Kenzie are at the wharf having a bite to eat. I could walk you both down there and we could meet them?"

Now why had he offered that? He knew that Ana had lived on the island for at least eight years while her husband was stationed in the navy. She probably knew exactly where the wharf was.

"That'd be great. Thanks, Ian. I desperately need to run inside and use the bathroom first, though." She paused. "Do you mind keeping an eye on Emily?"

Alarm slid through him and his mouth flapped a bit. She was trusting him with a child? As in babysitting?

"I, well—"

"Five minutes." Ana laughed and patted him on the shoulder. "You'll be fine. She'll probably keep doing flips the whole time I'm gone."

And then Ana disappeared into the house, leaving him alone with Emily.

But instead of doing flips and keeping her distance, Emily approached. Then, just a few feet from him, she kicked herself into a handstand.

"So how do you know my mom?" she asked, from upside down.

Oh boy. Not going there. "We were friends when she lived on the island."

"Were you her boyfriend?"

He mumbled something she wouldn't hear. *Shite, man, change the topic.*

"So how long have you been doing gymnastics, Emily?"

"Four years. I love it." She fixed her ponytail, which was falling down. "This is a great yard. We don't have a yard right now. We live in an apartment and there's nowhere to practice my gymnastics. I hate it."

"I'm sorry." And he was. Emily was obviously an energetic kid who needed lots of space to run around.

"It's okay. Mom says with the money we get from selling this house we can maybe buy a new one." She glanced around. "But I like this house. I wonder if we could live here."

That nearly had him guffawing out loud. Sarah moving to the island permanently? Not likely. She'd probably faint at the idea.

"You seem nice," Emily said lightly.

Nice wasn't generally a word that people described him with, but all right.

"Uh, well, thank you?"

"You're welcome."

"Neil was a real asshat."

Ian blinked, nearly choking on a reply. Had this child just referred to her father—by his first name at that—as an asshat?

"An asshat, you say? Do you even know what that means, Emily?"

"No. But I heard some teenagers call a mean guy an asshat at the mall once." She came out of the handstand and landed back on her feet.

Damn, she really was good. And she amused him. He almost found himself eager to hear what she'd say next, because there sure didn't seem to be any boundaries.

"I think that's why my mom divorced him. Because he was so mean. He made her cry." She strode forward, closer to him. "Do you make girls cry?"

Ouch. He struggled with the guilt over having made Sarah cry in the past, and the brewing fury that her husband had also brought her to tears.

"Not intentionally," he finally answered cautiously.

"Intentionally? Does that mean like on purpose?"

"Yes."

"That's good then." She spun away and did a series of cartwheels. "And you shouldn't hit girls either."

A chill swept through him at her seemingly casual words, but he could sense the intensity behind them. Anger. As if she'd witnessed something no child should have had to.

Fuck, what kind of asshat—as Emily put it—had Sarah married?

He wanted to ask if she'd ever seen her dad hit Sarah. It was on the tip of his tongue. But he didn't have the right. Emily was just a child.

"Aye, hitting is quite bad."

"You talk funny. Are you from England?"

"Scotland. Long ago, though. Most of my accent is gone now."

"I still hear it." Emily returned to his side. "It's pretty."

Lovely. He had a pretty voice.

His lips quirked and he glanced furtively toward the house. Where the hell was Ana, and what was taking her so long?

"So, uh, how do you do in school?" he asked conversationally.

"I do good in school, but it's so boring."

"Yeah. It can be."

"You're not supposed to say that. You're supposed to tell me it's fun and it's good for me. Don't you know anything about being an adult?"

"Hmm. Apparently not." He shook his head. "You're a rather smart little girl, aren't you?"

She placed a hand on her hip and gave him a look of disgust. "I'm not a little girl, I'm a tween."

What the hell was a tween?

"Gonna be a teenager in three more years." She turned

away and did another cartwheel, sending her sunglasses flying.

Three? Wait. What? Ian paused, wracking his mind for that conversation he'd had with Sarah a few days ago. Hadn't she said Emily was eight?

"Five more, right?"

"No, I'm ten now. Ten plus three is thirteen. You should totally know that." She picked her sunglasses off the ground and slipped them back on, but not before he'd seen the vibrant green of her eyes.

Ian reared back, almost stumbling over his feet. His heart pounded twice as fast and the gears in his mind were cranking.

She was ten years old, not eight.

It wouldn't be the first time you forgot a condom.

Sarah's words raced through his head. The condom they'd forgotten on prom night.

No. She wouldn't have. There was no way Sarah would hide this from him. No way…

"What month is your birthday?" he rasped.

"February."

One word. And it changed his entire world.

Chapter Thirteen

"T HIS ISN'T HAPPENING." Sarah reread the text on her phone, struggling to even see the words because her hands were shaking so badly.

Emily and I are on the island. Just arrived at your house. And Ian's here, interestingly enough. We'll come down to the wharf shortly.

"We need to go." Shoving her phone back in her purse, she scrambled up from her seat. "Now."

"Why? What's up?" Kenzie grabbed her coffee and followed suit.

Her mom was messing with her, right? Only her mom wasn't a prankster by any means. Which meant Emily and her mother really *were* at Gran's house just up the road. And, apparently, Ian was with them.

She increased her stride, her stomach churning as she practically ran out of the building and back down the wharf.

"Hold on already?" Kenzie struggled to keep up. "Sarah, you look like you're about to puke. What is it? Emily? Is she hurt?"

"No. She's here."

"Oh. Really?" Confusion clouded her friend's tone. "Is that such a bad thing? I mean I know you didn't plan on her coming out, but Whidbey is a fun place for kids."

Kenzie had no idea. Was completely clueless of the potential damage control Sarah was facing.

They were just blocks from the house when she spotted them. Ian, Emily and her mother were walking side by side down the street toward them.

Her stomach heaved as she noted the way Emily seemed to be chatting a mile a minute. The closer they got, more nauseous Sarah became. Her mother looked almost stunned, and Ian...

Oh. Fuck.

He knew.

Outwardly, Ian didn't look too upset, but she knew him well enough to read the signs. The tension in his shoulders and the way he stared her down. If his gaze could shoot bullets she'd be bleeding to death right now.

"Mom!" Emily broke free from her grandma and ran the short distance that separated them, throwing herself into Sarah's arms.

"Hey, baby." She clung to her, squeezing probably much tighter than she should've.

"Grandma said we were going to come out here and surprise you. Make it a mini vacation."

"I'm...surprised." She lifted her head and stared at her

mom. *How could you?* she asked silently.

The guilt on her mother's face showed she'd known exactly what she was doing. What she'd risked.

"So, you're Emily?" Kenzie asked brightly, as oblivious to the tension among the group as Emily was. "You must be Sarah's daughter who I've heard so much about."

"Yeah." Emily nodded and pulled away from Sarah, but still gripped her hand. She stared up at Kenzie curiously.

"Well aren't you pretty?" Kenzie grinned. "You've got that long pretty hair, just like your mom. And those green eyes... Wow, you almost could pass for a McLaughlin..." Her voice trailed off and her brows knit. "Wait. How old are you?"

"She's ten," Ian said flatly.

Kenzie's gaze darted from Emily and then up to Ian, before finally moving back to Sarah.

"Sarah?" There was accusation in Kenzie's tone. Disbelief.

The world spun around Sarah. Bile rose sharply in her stomach as panic clawed at every inch of her being. Instinct had her trying to step around Ian, to rush to the house with Emily, but he stepped in front of her.

His green eyes—the same eyes as Emily—shimmered with a thin layer of shock, but more than that there was such a fierce rage that had her trembling.

"Kenzie, do me a favor and take Emily and Ana down to the ice cream shop for a cone." Ian's words were remarkably calm. Soft even. "I need to have a chat with Sarah for a bit."

Kenzie was quiet for a moment, still completely flummoxed. "I…ugh, yeah. I can do that. Do you like ice cream, Emily?"

"Do fish like water? Ugh, *yeah*, I do. Bring it on!" Emily tugged on Ana's hand. "Come on, Grandma."

Ana gave a slight nod and moved to take Emily's hand again.

"Mom, are you sure you don't want to come?" Emily asked.

More than anything. Actually, she wanted to grab her daughter and run like hell for the next ferry off the island.

She tried to speak past the lump in her throat. "You go and have fun. I'll spend time with you soon, Em."

"Okay."

Sarah didn't move. Likely couldn't have, as she watched the three trudge back down the street toward the ice cream shop.

Ian didn't say a word, but she could feel his stare. She nearly quaked under it.

"Ian—"

"Back to the house. We're not going to do this here."

He turned and strode back to the house, leaving her no choice but to follow.

Do this. She didn't even want to imagine what *do this* entailed. She'd feared this moment. Had gone almost eleven years without having to face it, and had naïvely assumed it would never occur.

And then one trip back to the island unraveled everything.

She wondered if being left the house, and its stipulation, had been part of a bigger plan of Gran's. That maybe it had very little to do with being left property, and everything to do with tying up loose ends between Sarah and Ian.

Gran, tell me this wasn't your plan all along.

Ian opened the door and let her walk in first before closing it behind him.

She wasn't sure what she expected. Not violence toward her. Not from Ian. But she didn't doubt he wanted to throw his fist through a wall or something.

"Why?" It was just one question, so heavy with disbelief and pain. A hard shrug accompanied it as he stared down at her.

She wasn't even sure how to answer. Struggled to find an acceptable one.

"You didn't tell me about my own child," he ground out. "She *is* my daughter, isn't she? I will hear the truth from your lips."

"Yes," she whispered. "Emily is your daughter."

"*Fuck.*" His curse was a roar that resonated through the house, and she cringed instinctively.

There was silence for a moment, heavy and swelling, as he paced the room and shook his head.

"You were so damn calculating. You flat-out told me she

was eight the other day. 'She's eight, almost nine.' You said it so casually, as if you weren't blatantly *lying*. You planned that, didn't you? If I asked."

"Yes." She couldn't deny it. That had been her plan for anyone on the island who asked.

It was why she didn't post pictures of her daughter online. Why she didn't even carry them in her wallet here. Emily had her frame, and she was on the smaller side. She *could* pass for eight, but those McLaughlin green eyes were a dead giveaway that he was her father.

"Did you feel no guilt at all for withholding the fact that the child in front of me was mine? That for eleven years you'd never bothered to tell me you got pregnant?"

"I *couldn't* tell you."

"Why? Because I was *nothing*? Because I was a pathetic excuse for a human? Because there would never be anyone more important in my life than myself?"

He threw all the words back at her with the same violence she'd once used to fling them at him. And they hit their mark. Shame sizzled through her again and she dropped her gaze.

Please, oh, please, she couldn't throw up. Even if her stomach was madly tossing around the dinner she'd eaten.

Those words were pretty awful. How had she ever said them that day, no matter how furious or hurt she'd been?

"Tell me. Did you know you were pregnant when you left the island?"

"No. I didn't find out until shortly after arriving in Japan."

"And it never occurred to you that I might want to know?" he snarled. "All this time. I had so much guilt for being an arsehole. For having a fling with our friend that I can't even remember." He shook his head. "But this is so much worse. This is *my child*."

The horror and devastation on his face were hard to see, and the guilt rising in her throat threatened to choke her.

"I hated you when I left." It was a shitty explanation, but it was the only one she had. "My dad kept telling me I couldn't trust you, and that you wouldn't have been able to handle being a father."

"Your dad would tell you anything to turn you against me. He hated me!"

"He was trying to do what was best for me and Emily. You would've resented having a child thrust on you."

"*No.* Don't speak for me, Sarah. Don't be my voice." He strode forward, the look on his face so savage she stumbled backward against the wall. "Fucking hell, you already made a choice for me that you had to no right to make. I would never have turned my back on my kid. If you knew me at all, you would've realized that."

Yes. She did know that. Now. She hadn't been in the emotional place to process it at the time. But after Emily was born and life had settled down a bit, it had sunk in.

Family was everything to the McLaughlins. Of course

Ian would have wanted to know. And she'd nearly told him at one point.

She trembled at his proximity. Her lashes fluttered closed—which only made it worse as she breathed in the familiar scent of him. He consumed her with his fury.

"I almost called you," she choked out. "Emily had just turned one, and I had started to regret not telling you. Not giving you the chance to see how amazing our little girl was. I wanted you to at least decide if you wanted to be a part of her life."

His hand closed over her shoulder and then he trailed his fingers toward her neck.

"You're killing me. Every word out of your mouth is killing me," he muttered raggedly, his thumb sweeping over the rapid pulse in her neck. "What stopped you from calling me?"

He wouldn't hurt her. Still, she knew, even though she could sense the violence barely leashed inside him.

The lump in her throat grew. "My dad. He discovered I was going to contact you, and handed me a printout of a background check on you."

She opened her eyes and watched realization flicker on his face, and then the dejection.

"Ah. So you knew I had a felony on my record before I told you the other day."

"Yes. And when I learned...I had to think of Emily, not just myself. Maybe it sounds horrible, but it reaffirmed I'd made the right choice by deciding to raise Emily by myself."

"But you didn't raise her by yourself, did you?" He laughed harshly and thrust away from her, as if he couldn't stand to be near her anymore. "You married some other sucker and told Emily he was her dad."

Some other sucker. Ouch. The blows kept coming. *And you deserve them.*

"No. I mean, yes to part of it. I married someone else my dad introduced me to. But I never led Emily to believe he was her dad."

"Ah. Which would be why she refers to him as Neil. How convenient."

She blinked away the tears that burned, because she would not cry right now. Though, oh Lord, she was so close to it. He had no idea what she'd been through.

"My life was anything but convenient," she said quietly, reaching the threshold for his verbal attack. Whether it was deserved or not. "Whether you believe me or not, my life was a personal hell."

&

IAN COULDN'T HIDE another laugh of dismay.

Oh that was just grand. Sarah was trying to make herself into a victim. What a surprise. Or not really.

Nothing could surprise him much at this point.

It really didn't get much worse than discovering you'd been chatting to a ten-year-old child who turned about to be the *daughter you'd never known about.*

He couldn't even bring himself to reply to what could only be Sarah's attempt at getting his pity. Right about now pity was the last emotion he felt for her.

His emotions toward her ran the gauntlet. Something so close to hate vibrated through him, but beneath it, barely breathing, was the ember of that hopeless ache for her that linked them.

Even vulnerable, distraught and visibly close to tears she was lovely. And so delicate.

Despite his rage, there was still that confounding gut-level instinct to want to comfort her. To pull her into his arms and hold her. To do what he could to take away the distress and guilt from her face. To forgive her.

Which is how you know you've drunk the Kool-Aid, mate.

Sarah didn't deserve his pity. She didn't deserve anything from him but disgust.

Had he ever really known her? How could he have loved—and thought he was falling in love with again—a woman who could keep such a massive, life-changing secret from him?

"Ian, you were never supposed to know." Her words sounded half-arsed now. As if she just wanted him to say it was okay and that he could understand why she'd done what she had.

He doubted he would ever be okay, but as much as he hated to admit it, he *could* almost understand her choices.

Could see her how she'd rationalized it.

Who wanted their kid to have a felon for a father?

"It's why I didn't bring her to the island when I came. Why I've never come back until now," she continued. "If you'd never found out, you'd be oblivious."

"Oblivious through your doing. And unfortunately, I'm not oblivious anymore. I'm—" he shook his head, thrusting his fingers through his hair "—not even sure what the hell I am. Or who I am. Though, apparently, I'm a father."

Fuck it all. A manic laugh exploded from his throat and again he had to curl his hands into fists.

She shook her head and her voice was low as she said, "Listen, you don't have to keep saying that. I don't expect anything from you. I know you don't want kids."

"Now how the hell would you know that?"

Dismay flickered across her face. "Are you serious? You told me just this morning you didn't want any."

He dismissed her words with a wave of his hand. "It's habitual. I've said it for so long, it's just what I say."

That seemed to really take the wind from her sail. She reared back, fear flashing in her eyes now.

"I don't understand. What do you want from us, Ian? What do you want me to do?"

That was a loaded question. Christ, he didn't even know himself.

"I don't know, honestly. I need to think."

She nodded. "Me too."

This time he bit back the snort of disdain. "No. What could you possibly have to think about now? The ball is in *my* court, doll. You have no right to try and call the shots from here on out. Got it?"

The fear amplified in her eyes. "You're not going to take my daughter from me."

She moved quickly toward the front door, but he intercepted her—suspecting she was going to find Emily. He caught her arm and swung her back around with more momentum than needed and her body crushed against his.

Sarah tried to shove at his chest to get away, but he caught her wrists to keep her still. Her words still resounded in his head.

"Your daughter? Try *our* daughter. It's a reality you'd better bloody well start getting used to."

The fight left her in an instant and she gave a strangled sob. Instead of pulling away, her weight crumpled against him and her head brushed against his chest.

Instinct had him releasing a wrist and sliding a hand up her back. It was an unintended gesture of comfort as he struggled with his thoughts. Having her in his arms—broken and afraid—he was all too aware of himself as a man against her small, feminine frame.

It was too easy to remember them in bed together. To envision her surrender and cries of pleasure as she lay beneath him.

No. He clenched his jaw at the way his blood immediately began to heat. He needed to remember the circumstances. This wasn't just about him and Sarah. There was Emily now.

A sudden thought sent tension spiraling through him and he eased his hand up to the back of her neck. His fingers stroked in a gentle warning.

"Don't even think about leaving the island again, Sarah—of taking Emily and leaving."

She hesitated a bit too long for his liking, before she answered with a husky, "No, I wasn't going to."

"Because if you do," he continued, his tone soft and dark with warning, "I *will* track you down. And I promise I won't be happy."

Sarah lifted her head and met his gaze. Her eyes held a hint of despondency. "I won't leave. Besides, I can't break the conditions of inheriting the house. I'm here for the month."

Three more weeks? It was suddenly like sand slipping through an hourglass. A ticking clock before she planned to take Emily and leave him again.

That wouldn't happen. He'd drag her through every court if needed before he let that happen.

Caught in the crystalline blue of her eyes—and realizing he wouldn't find any answers there—he released her abruptly and strode toward the door.

"I can't be near you right now, Sarah, but we're nowhere near done discussing this."

Chapter Fourteen

IT WASN'T DUE to a natural disaster. There'd been no death in the family. But for the first time in years, the McLaughlin Pub was closed for business. At least it was for the next hour.

"You didn't have to do this." Ian sat at one of the round tables in the pub, hands folded on the polished wood surface.

"Aye, I did," Aleck murmured grimly as he set up a Skype session on his laptop with their parents across the pond. "Family first."

"Absolutely. Family first." Kenzie had placed herself to his right and would occasionally squeeze his shoulder.

Colin sat at his left, quiet and seeming deep in thought, but their gazes would meet and Ian could see his twin was disturbed by the news of the night.

"Besides, we don't get busy until near ten anyway," Aleck murmured. "All right. I think we've got them. Can you see and hear us all right, Da? Ma?"

"Aye." Their father nodded. "We can hear ya just fine, son."

Hit with a pang of guilt, Ian observed his parents with their mugs of steaming tea, sitting at the table in their kitchen.

Even though it had to be the wee small hours of the morning in Edinburgh, their parents looked alert and properly concerned.

"Hello, you two." Ian didn't have to force the slight smile, or his next words. "It's always lovely to see you both— even if it's on the laptop screen. And thank you for waking up to chat with us."

Their mother gave a loud, cheerful laugh. "Well, you send us a text calmly informing us we're grandparents of a ten-year-old, and aye, we'll wake up right early for the details."

"Aye, we will. I'm still trying to understand why the lass didn't tell you, Ian." Dismay shone clear on their father's face.

Kenzie snorted. "Join the club. I'm her best friend and she never once even hinted at the fact."

"Well, if she didn't find it important to tell the father of her child, it seems unlikely she'd spill the beans to you." Colin grinned and blew the wrapper off a straw at his sister, before plunking the straw into an iced beverage. "Even though I know you're good mates and all."

She crumpled the wrapper and tossed it back at him. "I'll thank you to keep your sarcasm to yourself, dork."

Ian's lips twitched. Ah, and this is why he loved his family. He would be an utter mess without them right now.

It was a Friday night, and they were having a family meeting. Ian would've never asked Aleck to close the bar on one of the busiest nights of the week during the summer season.

And in the end he hadn't needed to, because Kenzie had done it. She'd seen how torn up and angry he was. How much he needed advice and a thread of normalcy in his suddenly chaotic life.

Word had spread quickly among the McLaughlins about Emily.

After leaving Sarah's, Ian had found Kenzie and asked her to get the word out to the family and see if anyone had a free moment. The most he'd been hoping for was a few minutes of their time to garner some advice.

He should've known better. His family always rallied for one another. Aleck had texted their parents, and hung a sign on the door that said the bar would be closed until nine p.m. due to a family emergency.

And now here they all were in a family meeting at the pub. It certainly wouldn't have been the first time, but since their parents had moved back to Scotland, they'd turned to relying on technology to keep everyone together.

"How are you doing with this discovery, Ian?" Their mother's brows were knit with concern, but even through the screen he could see the faint sparkle of excitement.

She obviously was pleased at the notion she had a grandkid, no matter how frustrating the discovery.

"Not so well, honestly." Ian's attention was snagged by the whisky his brother sat down in front of him. "Though this'll help. Thank you, Aleck."

"Any time."

"What is her name again? The girl?" his mother asked.

"Emily."

"And she's ten?" As if the seal had been broken, their mother launched into a torrent of questions. "Do you have a picture? I'll bet she looks like you. Is she just the sweetest thing?"

"Ma, easy there." Kenzie sighed. "She has the McLaughlin green eyes that we all got from Da. But other than that she's the spitting image of Sarah."

"I've no pictures yet, but I'm sure I can get some from Sarah." The words felt so odd on Ian's tongue.

They were talking about his daughter. He had a kid. The whole notion was still a complete mind-fuck.

"She's absolutely adorable and loads of fun," Kenzie added. "I'm already smitten with my niece and I've only known about her for a few hours." Her face lit up and she squealed suddenly, bouncing in her seat. "Oh wow, it's still sinking in. I'm an aunt!"

Colin heaved a sigh. "Are you all right there, Kenzie? Did you hurt something?"

"No, I didn't hurt something," she said tartly. "Forgive me, but the novelty hasn't worn off that I have a niece. And it likely won't wear off for several months. So you all might want to brace yourselves for more of these little episodes."

"I like that word. Episode. Reminds me of tantrum," Aleck teased. "You were good at those as a child too."

Kenzie made a face and tossed her hair over her shoulder. "I tell you, it'll be good to have another female in the mix. It's not easy with the lot of you boys." She glanced at the computer. "No offense, Ma, but you being in Scotland again certainly tips the scales."

Their mother laughed. "None taken, darling. And we really do miss you all."

Ian had been following the exchange with some amusement, and growing wonder. The entire family seemed to have accepted Emily being his daughter far easier than he had.

"So what are you going to do now?" their father asked.

"I don't know what to do," Ian finally admitted. "Where to go from here."

"You could hire a lawyer and fight for custody," Aleck suggested lightly.

Yes, and he'd considered it. He could already imagine the shock and fear on Sarah's face if he went forward with that plan of action. She'd likely try to castrate him on the spot.

But would she fight him if he wanted partial custody? Would a lawyer even be necessary?

"Well, what do you want? Do you want to take on the

SHELLI STEVENS

responsibility of being a father?" Colin glanced at him. "You've never seemed all that fond of kids before."

"No. I don't suppose I was. I didn't hate them, but I never went out of my way to cuddle a baby either." He gave a faint smile. "And yet, now it seems I have a child."

"Just crazy." Kenzie sighed. "I never thought you'd be the first one of us to become a parent."

Aleck pulled out his chair across the table and sat down. "The first ten years you were denied the chance to help raise Emily. But you have every right to fight for the chance to do so from here on out."

"Sarah didn't seem to want me in Emily's life up to this point," he pointed out flatly. "I can't imagine she'll be thrilled to have me start playing the role of dad now."

"But you *are* her da," his father protested, his voice rising. "It's not right that you weren't told."

There were murmurs of agreement around the table.

"Are you going to answer the question?" Aleck prodded. "Do you want to be part of her life?"

Ian tightened his grip around his glass and stared at his whisky.

Maybe he'd never been the father type, or imagined himself with kids, but now that he knew there was a child out there with his blood...well, it completely changed everything.

Emily was a physical presence in his life now. She was warm and vibrant, a bit random and shockingly blunt. He

198

could see reflections of himself in her. She was a part of him.

Just thinking about missing the first ten years of her life wrapped a fist around his heart and squeezed.

He didn't want to send her away and pretend he'd never found out. He couldn't. There was no way in hell he would ever make that choice. What he wanted was the chance to know her better.

"Aye." He finally gave a small nod. "I want to be a part of her life."

Pride flickered in their father's eyes. "Then you make it clear to Sarah that you want to be involved."

There was another chorus of ayes around the table, and words of support.

"I know what she did wasn't right, son." Their mother sighed. "But you'll need to keep a calm head upon you from this point out. I can't imagine you reacted very well."

"No. Not at all."

"Well, I sure as fook don't blame him," Aleck muttered.

"Nor I." Colin nodded. "Well, for the most part. You didn't hit her or anything of the sort, did you? Because you know I'll have to arrest your arse."

"Christ, no. What kind of man do you take me for, you bastard?"

Colin grinned. "One who doesn't always hold his temper. Though the few times you've lost it, I can't say that I blamed you."

They both glanced at Kenzie, but she dropped her gaze,

seeming to want no part of this turn in conversation.

"Is there anything between you and Sarah, or the possibility of anything?" their dad asked, a flicker of curiosity in his eyes. "I hear she's divorced."

"Aye, she is." Ian hesitated, not sure he wanted to dump the details of what sort of relationship he and Sarah had had since she'd returned to the island.

Especially seeing that it was primarily sexual.

Yet now there was Emily.

"I don't right know, to tell you the truth. There will always be *something* between us, but is it enough?"

"I think it is. Add in a child you both have, then yes," their mother chimed in.

"Whatever road you choose, Ian, you know we'll always support you."

Ian met Aleck's steady gaze, and then nodded at the firm words.

"Thank you. All of you. A man could truly not ask for a better family."

"Agreed. Well, I suppose this family meeting is wrapped up then?" Their father asked, glancing at his wife.

"Aye. Call it a night, already," Ian agreed. "You're likely half asleep, Da."

"After drinking this tea? I'm on a caffeine high and doubt I'll sleep anytime soon." He kissed his wife's cheek and laughed. "But I'm sure your mother and I can figure out a way to entertain ourselves."

"Thank you for that thought, Da," Kenzie hollered. "Now let me just find a bucket to throw up in."

"I want pictures of my grandchild," their mother pleaded. "And if you could find out her size in clothing, what her favorite color is, what her favorite toys are—"

"Oh jeez, she's bent on spoiling the grandchild she's only known about for a few hours!" Colin guffawed.

Kenzie rolled her eyes. "Aye, well she'll have to get in line."

Ian laughed and shook his head. "Love you all."

Everyone chimed in with fond responses, and a moment later Aleck ended the session.

"Well? How are you feeling about where you go from here?"

Ian considered everything they'd discussed and weighed his emotions and the status of his heart.

"I feel pretty decent," he murmured, almost surprised to realize he did. "Optimistic even. Thank you all again."

"No need for thanks—we're family." Aleck pushed back his chair and stood. "I hereby call this McLaughlin family meeting adjourned."

Kenzie rose and rolled her eyes. "Gee, we've either landed in a courthouse or the eighteen-hundreds. Could you be any more formal, big brother?"

"Aye, I could." He kissed the top of her head. "Now let's get this pub open and start making some money."

"Well *I* hereby request a shot of whisky before we do

that." Kenzie moved to give Ian a hug. "It's been a long day."

Ian hugged his sister back tightly. Amusement, fondness and a deep appreciation for his family ran through him. He knew he'd been unusually quiet tonight, but his mind was elsewhere.

Kenzie pulled away and gave him a gentle smile. "Go sleep on this tonight, and see her tomorrow."

"That's my plan. Thank you, Kenzie, for all you did today."

"Anytime." She gave a small smile. "I owe you anyway."

"You don't owe me a thing." He squeezed her hand, then turned and left the pub.

∽

SARAH CRACKED OPEN a can of diet soda and handed it to her mom before settling down on the couch with her own soda.

Her mother sat at one end, her legs curled under her bottom, her gaze cast downward. She'd been like that most of the night—avoiding eye contact.

But now that it was pushing ten and Emily was asleep in the other room, Sarah wasn't about to avoid the topic any longer.

"What were you thinking, Mom? Coming out here?" She shook her head and tightened her fingers around the soda can. "Did you really think he wouldn't find out?"

"A child should be with her mother," Ana said firmly.

"We were making plans to come out even before you called and asked for the money. Emily wasn't happy in Florida."

"Yes, well sometimes she's not happy being forced to bathe either. You know how children work; you have two of them." She laughed softly, but it was without humor. "And then you left Ian alone with Emily today. You had to know what would happen then. That girl is a chatterbox. She probably gave him enough clues to put it together within five minutes."

"Yes, that was about how long it took," Mom agreed. "I was only in the house for maybe seven minutes total. And when I came out and saw the shock on his face, well, I knew he'd figured it out. And of course then I realized how badly I'd screwed up."

"You did. You really, really did. I made the decision to leave her with you in Florida to avoid this happening. This is pretty much my worst nightmare."

Ana was silent for a moment, seeming lost in thought. "Is he really so bad? Ian?"

How could she even answer that? Her mother had seen the same printout Sarah had that day when her father had shown them.

"He has a felony on record, remember?"

"I remember. Assault, wasn't it?"

"Second degree."

"Hmm. That's bad?"

"Well, I'm hardly a legal expert, but from what I understand only first degree is worse. And that kind of violence is a terrible example to Emily."

"Hmm." Ana sighed and stretched her legs out on the couch. "I always liked Ian. No matter that your father didn't."

Sometimes her mom was a hopeless romantic. "He broke my heart, Mom. I found him in bed with another girl. You have no idea how badly—"

"It hurts? I do. Your father wasn't perfect. No man is."

A beat went by as Sarah tried to process what her mom was saying. Had her father had an affair? The idea made her stomach roil.

"He was a sailor. He was gone a lot," her mom continued. "And one time the temptation was too much for him." Their gazes locked. "But I loved him enough to stay. To make it work. Because he loved us, and there wasn't anything he wouldn't do to protect us."

Sarah shook her head. "Dad had an affair? When was this?"

"When you were around seven, and your sister had only just been born."

"I never knew."

Ana smiled faintly. "He never wanted you to. Once I forgave him, we agreed to never talk about it. We would never pass that stress or grief on to you girls. It was our burden."

"Well, you both carried it well. I didn't have a clue."

It was almost too hard to believe that her dad had been unfaithful. And yet, at the same time, it wasn't. Sarah had known he wasn't perfect. She'd hated the way he'd treated Ian and could be so hard-headed and stubborn when he deemed himself right. But he'd been her dad. Protective and loving and she hated thinking badly of him. And in the end, he'd been right about Ian, hadn't he?

"I didn't tell you this to taint your father's memory, Sarah. I only thought it might help you understand that sometimes love is worth fighting for."

"You sure didn't seem to feel this way at the time when Ian and I split up."

"No, you're right. I didn't," Ana agreed. "At the time you were so young. Not even eighteen. I thought it was puppy love that would quickly fade. Harmless."

Never had Sarah ever once written off what had been between her and Ian as puppy love. They'd been young, yes. Probably even naïve. But their love had been all too real.

"When you talk about each other, I see it." Her mom's expression turned pensive. "When he would mention you, or you him, it's there. That sparkle of someone who's in love."

That sparkle isn't love, Mom. Just the remains of two people who've recently gotten their rocks off with each other. Sarah bit the inside her cheek so she wouldn't say the words aloud. Even if they were on the tip of her tongue.

Instead, she murmured, "I don't think it's love, Mom. Besides, that boat has sailed."

"Then you swim out to it."

Her heart skipped a beat at the intensity of her mother's statement. The connotation behind it.

Swim out to it.

There was so much bitter history between them, creating a strong riptide that would make it pretty damn hard to reach that boat. Even if she wanted to.

And right now, she didn't know what she wanted anymore.

"I know love. And I think you two have a chance."

Before Sarah could reply, there was the soft padding of footsteps.

"Mom?" Emily appeared in the living room, eyes bleary from sleep. "Can I sleep with you tonight? I had a nightmare."

Her heart melted a little and she gave a small nod. Even though her daughter touted her tweenhood, sometimes she couldn't fight the fact she was a momma's girl.

"Come on." She stood and followed Emily into the bedroom. She'd missed Emily more than she thought during the week apart.

She couldn't let Ian take Emily. Not that she thought he really would, but the idea of it. The what if. It would destroy her.

～

SARAH STARED AT the outside of McLaughlin's Auto and

Classic Car Restoration and hesitated. She tightened her fingers around the plate of chocolate chip cookies and drew in a slow breath.

Get some courage, girl. You need to do this.

Lifting her head, she strode forward and into the office section of the shop. A small bell rang as she entered, and the young woman behind the counter glanced up.

"Good morning. What can I help you with?"

"Actually, I was hoping to see Ian?"

The young woman stood. "I'll check and see if he's available. Who can I tell him is here?"

"Sarah. He'll know who I am." Whether he'd see her or not was another story.

"Aye. I know her."

Both women glanced over at Ian as he came out of the office and shut the door.

Sarah drew a sharp breath in as her pulse quickened.

"You didn't need to come in." His tone was flat, a clear contradiction to the glittering anger in his eyes. "I told you I'd contact you when I was ready."

The receptionist made a squeak of surprise and excused herself, disappearing into the garage area where several men were working.

A blush of embarrassment stole up her neck, but Sarah kept her chin high. "I know. I just brought you cookies."

That sounded pretty lame.

"You brought me cookies?"

been hoping to get hurt and humiliated.

Which, no, that absolutely hadn't been her goal. But again her naïveté was showing.

Increasing her pace and blinking back the tears that burned, she made her way back home.

༄

"THANK YOU FOR dinner. This lasagna is delicious, but it's going to go straight to my hips."

Sarah laughed and gave her mom a sideways glance. "You could use some padding on your hips. You're too skinny. And I swear if Emily hears you talk like that you'll give her a complex."

"Oh I will not—that kid is tiny." Ana pushed her plate away and made a sound of disbelief. "And she's in the bedroom watching the Disney channel again anyway."

"Yes, well, she's at that age and the girls in her gymnastics class are always talking about dieting."

"Ridiculous."

"I agree." Sarah took another bite of her dinner, but she still had no appetite. Her stomach had been in knots since leaving Ian's garage earlier this afternoon.

They'd had a late dinner after driving around the island and exploring various places with Emily. They'd watched the sunset from the porch of the house, before everyone came inside to eat.

A satisfying day, she reflected. For the most part. Her

heart grew heavy as she replayed the brief encounter with Ian.

"So he wasn't receptive to the cookies?"

Her mom always had a knack for knowing where her mind had gone.

"I'm sure he was fine with the cookies. Seeing me, however…"

"Give him time."

Oh how she wished time were the answer. But forgiveness wasn't always the easiest pill to swallow. She knew firsthand how strong a hold pain and anger could have on you.

A soft knock came at the door, sending tension racing through her.

Ana murmured lightly, "Speaking of. One guess who that'll be."

"I don't need to guess." Even without the porch light illuminating his recognizable stature, Sarah knew Ian was the person knocking on her door.

"Go take a walk with him. Or a drive. I'll watch Emily while you two talk." Ana gave a small shudder of excitement. "I'll just watch an episode of *Castle* on my laptop—my friend Joyce got me hooked on it. That Nathan Fillion is such a hunk."

That last comment caused a reluctant smile as Sarah opened the door. Seeing Ian leaning against the doorjamb, staring down at her with that familiar scowl on his face, had her smile fading.

Classic Car Restoration and hesitated. She tightened her fingers around the plate of chocolate chip cookies and drew in a slow breath.

Get some courage, girl. You need to do this.

Lifting her head, she strode forward and into the office section of the shop. A small bell rang as she entered, and the young woman behind the counter glanced up.

"Good morning. What can I help you with?"

"Actually, I was hoping to see Ian?"

The young woman stood. "I'll check and see if he's available. Who can I tell him is here?"

"Sarah. He'll know who I am." Whether he'd see her or not was another story.

"Aye. I know her."

Both women glanced over at Ian as he came out of the office and shut the door.

Sarah drew a sharp breath in as her pulse quickened.

"You didn't need to come in." His tone was flat, a clear contradiction to the glittering anger in his eyes. "I told you I'd contact you when I was ready."

The receptionist made a squeak of surprise and excused herself, disappearing into the garage area where several men were working.

A blush of embarrassment stole up her neck, but Sarah kept her chin high. "I know. I just brought you cookies."

That sounded pretty lame.

"You brought me cookies?"

"Well…for you to share with your shop." This was a bad idea. Why had she thought it would be a good attempt at chipping away at his icy anger? "They're chocolate chip. Emily and I baked this morning, and you did say I could bake something as payment for the car…" She trailed off lamely and bit back a sigh. "Though I fully intend to pay you still."

"I see." He didn't even crack a smile as he took the plate from her. "I'm sure my guys will love them."

But not him. Why was every word like a blow to her heart? A lump gathered in her throat and she tried to give a small smile, but it didn't quite stay put.

"Look, you shouldn't have come." His words were terse. "I'm working and I'm just not…ready to deal with you yet."

Deal with her.

She might have flinched, but his bluntness actually helped her realize what was going on in his head. "Understood."

"I've got things to do." His gaze swept over her, almost reluctantly, before his expression grew hard. "Thanks for the cookies. I'll be sure to return the plate."

"All right."

He turned away and strode back into his office. The door slammed shut a moment later.

Sarah made haste getting the hell out of his shop and away from the stares that followed her.

So maybe the cookies weren't a good idea—unless she'd

Chapter Fifteen

"**H**I."

He answered with a small nod. "Can I come in?"

"Do you mind if we walk? It'll give us more privacy, and it's warm enough out." She stepped outside on the porch and closed the door behind him. "Unless you'd rather drive somewhere?"

"No. Walking is fine." He fell into step next to her as they walked out of the driveway. "I've felt a bit restless today anyway."

"Understandable."

Restless was probably the most passive emotion he'd felt, she guessed. There'd been a good amount of rage last night that had lingered into this afternoon.

Where had he gone yesterday after he'd left here? He must've taken time alone to think. Or maybe he'd met up with one of his siblings. Maybe Colin, since they were pretty close.

She snuck a sideways glance at him in the growing darkness. It was surprising how relaxed he was now. Such a one-eighty from this afternoon. The raw edge of fury and shock had evaporated. If anything, he just seemed tired.

Sarah swallowed the guilt and thrust her hands into her jeans pockets.

"Thanks for the cookies—they were good. If you could pass that on to Emily…"

"I will." *So awkward.* "I'm glad you liked them."

More silence. Heavy and uncomfortable. He broke it first.

"You didn't run. I mean, obviously."

"I told you I wouldn't." Though when he'd left last night, the side of her that was in full-blown panic mode had considered it. Until logic had stepped in. "Cat's out of the bag now anyway, right?"

"Right. Or kid."

Was that an attempt at humor? The slight quirking of his lips made her think maybe it was.

"Yeah. Or kid."

More silence as they walked down toward Main Street. It was pretty quiet with most of the businesses closed, except for a small bar that had been around forever.

She cast him another sideways glance. His stride was easy and there was none of the tension in his shoulders that she'd become accustomed to in the last couple of days.

"You seem calmer tonight."

"I've had time to think about it—to let my heels cool.

We need to move forward from here and my staying angry or bitter will do us little good. Which my family helped me realize when I talked things over with them last night."

She sucked in a quick breath as tension coiled through her. "Oh? All your family?"

"Aye."

Meaning his parents had probably been involved in the discussion somehow too. Maybe he'd called them. Were they disappointed in her? Just as angry as Ian had been?

The possibility bothered her more than it should've. She'd adored them, and only now was it really sinking in that by not telling Ian, she'd also denied his parents the right to know their grandchild. Kenzie and his brothers the right to be an aunt and uncles.

"Does everyone hate me?" She tried to keep her voice flat and casual, but the crack in it betrayed her vulnerability.

He didn't answer right away, and her heart quickened.

"No one hates you, Sarah. Despite what happened between us and how bitterly we ended, they've always adored you." He paused. "Though they're confused and unhappy that you chose to hide Emily from us."

She nodded, unable to argue with that. Emotion gathered and tightened her throat. Decisions she'd made so long ago now seemed rash and selfish.

"I somewhat understand why you did what you did," he said quietly. "We were both young. I'm sure you thought of me as a troublemaker who couldn't even be faithful half a year into dating. And when you decided to try and give me a second chance, you discovered I had a criminal record. I may not like what you did, but trust me, I get it."

Her throat tightened with emotion. That was it. Pretty much exactly it. And then add in the constant pressure from her dad, and it had been so much easier to just go with the flow than swim against the current.

They had walked out onto the wharf and he stopped halfway to the end. Gripping the railing, he stared out over the water.

She didn't speak, because she knew he needed to unload. Needed to tell his side of things and where he was at now.

Again, he fell into silence, though. She traced her fingers over the ridges in the wooden railing and turned her gaze to the water as well.

The moon had risen and reflected in a shimmery opalescent circle on the water.

"Here's the thing." He sighed, and she heard the heaviness in it. "I can't walk away from Emily now that I know of her existence. No matter how unfit you may think I am as a father, it doesn't change that fact that I'm Emily's dad."

Her heart quickened and she took tiny breaths in. She'd half expected it, but hearing him saying the words aloud, so casually almost, was surreal.

Surely at any moment she'd wake up and find it had all been a crazy dream.

But, no. This was happening.

He turned slightly to face her and she did the same, until they were just inches apart and their gazes met and held.

"I want to be part of her life. And I want you to tell her exactly who I am."

She couldn't reply. Couldn't seem to focus on anything except the rushing in her ears.

He wanted to be in her life. How much of a part?

"I don't...how do we even..." She shook her head. "We live in Virginia."

"Aye. You do. But it's summer, Emily's out of school, and you have a house here that you've just inherited."

She blinked, shock sliding through her. "Are you asking me to move back to the island?"

"No. Well perhaps consider it in the future. Right now, all I'm asking is that you stay through the summer. Give me a chance to get to know my daughter."

Stay through summer. Her head spun with the idea. It wasn't impossible. In fact, it was a downright reasonable request. A little nerve-racking, but reasonable.

"Okay, we can do that. And I agree that we should probably tell Emily you're her dad, but how do you think we should go about it?"

How did you introduce your child to the father she'd never met?

"Did she ever ask about me? About who her real father was?"

"Occasionally, yes. When she was younger I told her that

you lived in another state and just weren't a part of our lives. It seemed to be enough."

"And as she grew older?"

"Well, then it wasn't enough. She wanted to know who you were and why you weren't around."

She winced at the sharp breath he drew in, and then the string of soft curses he dropped.

"And what did you say then?"

"I said I would tell her the whole story when she was old enough to understand. And then I'd change the topic." She let out a humorless laugh. "I got great at diverting conversations."

"I bet."

Ouch.

"Sorry. I'm trying. Trying to let go of the anger, but it's going to come out now and then." He turned to look out over the water again. He thrust a hand through his hair and shook his head. "I just don't want to wait to tell her. She's gone ten years without knowing who her father is, and I'd rather not waste any more time dancing around it."

Her heart started thumping double time, as the scene of how that would go down played in her head. Just the idea of doing it made her stomach hurt.

"Look, my family is heading out to the Highland Games tomorrow in Bellingham. Why don't you bring Emily and come have some fun? She can meet everyone, watch us do our thing and then we'll spend some time together."

"And then?"

"Then we'll see how it goes. If the moment feels right, we'll tell her."

The Highland Games. Of course Ian would be going. The McLaughlins traveled to all the somewhat local ones— even some non-local ones. And the family had always been incredibly popular at them. There had even been a fan base of young girls that followed the brothers around.

"Okay," she agreed, because what else could she say? "And at the end of the summer? What then?"

Why had she just asked that? Was she insane? She couldn't even imagine tomorrow, let alone two months from now.

But when she risked another glance at Ian, she found him watching her again. This time his expression had changed, become more considering. As if he'd just thought of something.

Which made her wonder if he was getting any crazy ideas.

∿

IAN DIDN'T EVEN want to contemplate the end of summer. Really, he couldn't. Right now was more than enough to focus on.

"I don't right know what happens after the end of summer," he confessed. "Let's just take it one day at a time."

His words did little to ease Sarah's troubled gaze, and

because he'd wanted to do it for the last few moments, he reached out to trace his fingers over the pale softness of one cheek.

Surprisingly, she didn't pull away and her lips even parted slightly. Resignation flared with the heat in her eyes, as if she realized, as he had, that fighting this passion between them was hopeless.

"Sarah," he murmured her name on a sigh.

Her eyes rounded and he was again sucked in by their dark intensity.

Alone together on the wharf, with the stars above them and their bodies so close, he couldn't help but be aware of her. To let his mind drift back to what it had been like to make love to her again.

To erase the bullshit experience he'd given her yesterday morning, and replace it with something more romantic.

Romantic? What the hell was wrong with him?

With every breath he drew in, there was the smell of salt and seaweed from Penn Cove, but there was the scent of lavender lotion that he would always associate with Sarah.

When she shivered, his attention shifted to her bare arms. He wasn't cocky enough to think it was all due to him. The tank top must not be keeping her warm—beneath the cotton he could see her nipples pressed taut.

"You're cold?"

"A little," she mumbled, before her gaze slipped away.

"Here." Shrugging out of the flannel he wore over a T-shirt, he placed it around her shoulders.

"You'll be cold," she protested, even as she slipped her arms into it.

"I don't get cold easily. Too much body fat." He deftly fastened the buttons on the shirt.

She made a soft snort of derision likely at his unwarranted fat joke, but it ended on a gasp when his fingers brushed the swell of her breast.

This time, when he met her gaze, there was nothing but desire in her eyes.

Ah fuck it all. With his fingers still holding his shirt, he used it to tug her closer.

Her hands came up between them, resting on his stomach as her head tilted up toward his. Her mouth parted in an offering maybe she wasn't even aware of.

Whether it was a good idea or not, Ian took it. He lowered his head and kissed her.

First just a taste. A reminder of the soft fullness of her mouth that he'd always loved. And then, when she made that breathy little sigh, he dipped his tongue past her lips to drink deeper.

So sweet. Almost intoxicating. It had always been like this when they'd kissed. He'd become drunk on her mouth.

His body stirred to life, but he struggled to control it. They couldn't take this too far. Sarah had to get back to Emily soon.

But for now, for a few more minutes, he could enjoy her.

Enjoy the moment. He loved the gentle way her tongue sparred with his, and the way the tips of her breasts just barely touched his chest.

When they pulled apart a few minutes later, he drew in a long, unsteady breath. She laid her head against his chest, and he folded her tighter into his arms.

It felt so good to hold her like this. Without anger. Without motivation.

"We're good this way."

"What do you mean?"

"Physically. We work really well together." His mind latched on to the idea. "We shouldn't write the possibility of us off."

"I don't know." Wariness crept into her words, but she didn't pull away. "It might just complicate things."

How could it complicate things? They'd already stepped in that puddle anyway by sleeping together. They already had a daughter together, and after their little slipup this morning, there was the possibility of another one.

An idea flashed through his head again, just as it had several minutes ago. At first he'd written it off as ridiculous, but it hadn't gone away. And the longer it fermented in his head it began to almost make sense.

"Sarah, maybe we should just get married."

Now she did pull away, and rather quickly. "Get married? What...? Where did that come from?"

"It's actually quite a brilliant solution, the more I think

about it." The idea gained momentum and he could hear his words grow more animated. "I mean the number one reason would be for Emily, but getting married wouldn't be so bad."

She tilted her head and said flatly, "Just a *little* bad, huh?"

"Look, we're amazing in bed. We likely even care about each other if we would stop being stubborn and admit it—"

"Ian…"

"A moment to finish my thoughts, doll. You're struggling financially, and I'm doing quite well right now. How can this not be a win-win solution? We should do it. Let's get married."

She stared at him, eyes narrowed again. "This is your idea of a proposal?"

"I, er, guess?" He chuckled at the thought of what his brothers would say if they could see him now. "It's funny, actually. I used to tell Colin that marriage was for suckers and that I'd never throw myself under that bus. But I would do it for you."

"Throw yourself under the bus?" she repeated with slow deliberation. "Marrying me would be equivalent to throwing yourself under a bus?"

"Yes. Wait, what?" Ian blinked and ran back in his head what he'd said. His excitement faded instantly.

Ah shite. He'd completely fucked this up.

"Um, would you believe that came out a bit wrong?"

"Yeah, I really would believe that." Her eyes flashed with anger, but there was a hint of amusement beneath. She pushed away from him and folded her arms across her chest. "Look, clearly you *suck* at proposing—not that I'd marry you anyway."

"You wouldn't?" Why did that make his heart sink a bit? "Why not?"

"Because we're not going to make good sex the foundation for marriage."

"Okay, but I gave a few other reasons."

"Emily, yes." She snorted. "And the other one basically being an offer to be my sugar daddy."

Hmm, yes, he'd blown the marriage topic completely.

"I have money—it's just tight right now with paying off a divorce."

Right. Of course she was right. About everything. But getting married had seemed to make perfect sense. And yet marriage did need more than all the asinine reasons he'd just listed, didn't it?

Not that he was one of those romantics who demanded love. Another random thought raced through his head.

"Out of curiosity, is that what you did before?" he asked. "When you married that Neil guy? Confuse good sex for love?"

Her irritation visibly faded into dismay, and then wariness flickered in her eyes before she answered. "No, not at all. I didn't even sleep with him until we were married. And after that it was just a handful of times."

Mind blown.

Ian watched, completely flummoxed as she turned to stare back out over the water.

Only a handful of times? How long had they been married? Seven or eight years? That had to be one of the reasons why the marriage had ended.

"You rarely had sex? But why? Was he terrible in bed?"

With the flow of conversation, it had been a natural question. Until he'd realized he didn't want the image of Sarah in bed with another man. The idea of it kind of made him want to punch something. Or someone.

She was silent for a moment. "It doesn't matter. I'd rather not talk about it, okay?"

Actually, that was quite fine with him. "Okay."

They fell into another silence. Who knew where her mind had gone, but his had managed to jump right back into the marriage idea.

Maybe it wasn't for the right reasons, but they had some compelling reasons, didn't they?

If he hadn't fucked up when they were first together, they would've probably been married by now anyway.

Guilt, heavy and familiar, gripped him at the thought of that night. It had become exhausting all the countless times he'd played it back in his head, trying to figure out where he'd gone wrong. When he'd made that choice to throw away everything he'd had with Sarah.

"I'll see if I can borrow Mom's rental car tomorrow, and drive up to Bellingham to see you guys."

Relief slid through him as he glanced at her—found a tiny smile playing around her mouth now.

"Aye?"

"Yes. Emily will love it. I always enjoyed the Highland Games." She met his gaze. "When we were dating I was so excited, waiting for summer to arrive so that I could hang out and watch you guys at all the games." Her lashes fluttered down. "And I would know half the girls in attendance would be jealous of me, because *I* was Ian McLaughlin's girlfriend."

His heart kicked up a notch at her soft admission, and the tiny seed of hope inside him grew an inch.

"I'm sorry we didn't make it 'til summer, because I would've loved having you there as my girl watching me, doll."

Was it his imagination, or did she blush at his last words? It was difficult to tell in the darkness.

"I hope you and Emily will cheer me on tomorrow."

"Yes, of course we will. We'll cheer for all the McLaughlins." She gave a half-smile. "I mean, that's half of who Emily is, right? Scotland is in her blood."

"Aye."

The intimacy of the conversation just made him more aware of her. Sarah. His lover then and now. The mother of his child. She looked so small and fragile wearing his shirt. So absolutely right.

I want her back.

The realization settled with a heavy finality. Not just for

a few nights in bed, but on a forever basis.

The thought alone was staggering and the implications overwhelming. But he didn't run from them. Instead he reached out and cupped her upper arm, turning her toward him again.

"I know I completely blew that attempt at proposing, but my intentions were good. Just promise me you'll consider it, all right?"

She didn't answer, and he sensed she was genuinely surprised.

"Sarah?"

Finally she gave a small nod. "Okay, but—"

Ian brushed his mouth over hers to steal away whatever protest she was trying to come up with.

Again she didn't pull away, and again it gave him hope. He tasted her deeply and thoroughly, until his body began to stir and his heart beat harder.

It was just another small taste, but he wanted it to tide him over until they had another night together. Because there would be another night, and soon.

He slowed the kiss, brushing his lips over hers one last time before he had to take her home. It wasn't their parents setting a curfew nowadays, but their daughter, Emily, who needed her mother.

"Think about it," he murmured against her lips. "Promise."

With a soft sigh, she promised again.

Chapter Sixteen

"THIS IS GOING to be so cool."

Sarah lifted her gaze to glance at Emily in the rearview. Her daughter was twisting again in her seat, obviously excited as she stared out the window at the passing trees.

"What's this thing we're going to called again?"

"The Highland Games."

"*Awesome*. Is it like the Hunger Games?"

Sarah laughed at the mention of the popular book-series-turned-movies that so many people loved.

"No, because then we'd have a bunch of men in skirts trying to kill each other."

Her daughter giggled. "Do the boys really wear those skirts?"

"Yes, some of them do. And I was kidding—they're not called skirts. They're called kilts."

"Have you been to the Highland Games, Mom?"

"Yes, but not for a long time. Since before you were born."

And now she was going again. Anxiety was a hardened knot lying in her belly. While her mom and Emily had devoured the banana pancakes and slices of thick bacon Sarah had made, she'd barely touched her food.

A couple bites of pancakes and three cups of coffee meant she was running on food fumes and a lot of caffeine to make the hour drive to Bellingham.

After Sarah had given her mom the update about today, Ana had decided to skip the Games and planned to spend a few days with an old friend who lived on the island.

"So, Em, what do you think of Ian?"

"The man from yesterday?" Emily shrugged. "He was nice, but not very good at math."

"What do you mean?"

"I told him I'd be a teenager in three years, and he thought I should've said five years. I mean, duh. The difference between thirteen and ten is totally three, not five."

Sarah stared at the road and frowned. Ian wasn't stupid; of course he knew how to subtract.

It clicked. He'd just been subtracting the wrong years. She'd told him Emily was eight. And if Emily made some kind of countdown to being a teenager comment—which she was becoming famous for—that's probably when he'd figured it out.

"I like Kenzie too. She let me get two scoops of ice cream, Mom. Chocolate peanut butter and bubble gum."

"Sounds…delicious." Or not. "We're going to spend

some time with all the McLaughlins today, Em."

"There's more of them here? Cool."

Oh just two uncles, one aunt, and your dad. By the end of the day Emily would know about them all.

Would she be upset? Be excited? Go all tween-drama on her? Or would Sarah be the only one a complete mess after the conversation?

When they were parked and walking toward the entrance to the games, her heart skipped a bit faster.

"Do you hear that?" Emily exclaimed, quickening her pace. "That's bagpipes, right?"

"Yes. Sounds like they're warming up."

Her phone buzzed in her purse and she dug it out to find a text from Ian.

> *I paid admission for you and Emily. Just give the man at the gate your names. I'll be at the caber toss when you get inside.*

"Who texted you, Mom?"

"Ian," she replied absently. "He paid our admission."

"Cool. Yeah, I definitely think he's pretty nice."

He was. He seemed determined to try and take care of her, even more so now that he knew Emily was his daughter.

Last night flashed through her head. He'd pretty much proposed out on the wharf. It had almost been comically endearing, and she hadn't taken him the least bit seriously. Until she'd realized he wasn't kidding a bit.

Then she couldn't have been more stunned if he'd pulled

out a ring. Well, okay, maybe that.

"Glad you girls made it."

Emily pulled away with a squeal and launched herself at Kenzie, who'd approached from the side.

Kenzie's eyes closed as she drew Emily into an embrace, squeezing tightly. And Emily hugged her back. As if she somehow sensed the connection.

Kenzie opened her eyes and met Sarah's gaze over Emily's head. There was no anger or condemnation in Kenzie's expression, but the disappointment there was almost worse.

Kenzie was another victim of her secret—she was obviously still coming to terms with the fact that Emily was her niece. Though she didn't say anything to Emily, which meant Ian had probably warned her that Emily didn't know yet.

Sarah attempted a half-smile. "We're excited to be here this morning to support you all."

"And I hear they have cool swords you can buy," Emily added and slid away from Sarah. "I like your outfit, Kenzie. It's so cool."

As always, Kenzie looked beautiful in the Highland Dance costume that consisted of a blue-and-red tartan kilted skirt, matching hose, and a white blouse with a black velvet vest over it.

Her makeup was darker than usual and her strawberry blonde hair was twisted up in a bun. Sarah could well understand why her daughter was enraptured. Just wait until she watched the dance competition.

"Do you get to do any games?" Emily asked.

"No, I'll not be doing any games, Emily, but I do dance. In fact, I was just on my way over. Would you like to come watch?"

"Yes, yes, yes! Can we go, Mom?"

"We wouldn't miss it."

Kenzie met her gaze again, and gave a faint smile. "Good. Let's head over then."

Sarah went to catch her daughter's hand, but Emily had already run up beside Kenzie to chat her ear off.

Obviously that ice cream yesterday had won Emily over. Though Sarah knew it was much more than that. Kenzie was a bright light that drew everyone to her. Not only was she beautiful, but she radiated fun and humor as well.

Soon Sarah and Emily were seated in the row in front of the small stage watching Kenzie and a handful of other women and girls dancing.

"This is so cool," Emily whispered.

It really was. Sarah had always enjoyed watching her friend dance. The art of Highland Dancing was fascinating. It almost seemed like an upbeat ballet. They danced on their toes, jumping and kicking to the bagpipes that played off stage.

The Highland Dance blended athleticism and grace, and the fast pace had Emily bobbing in her seat and her gaze locked on the dancers.

This was part of Emily's heritage, Sarah thought with growing realization, and she didn't even know it.

The hand that descended lightly on Sarah's shoulder made her jump and she glanced over her shoulder.

"Ian." She returned his small smile, flushing slightly at the intensity of his green stare.

"Good morning."

"Good morning." She tucked a strand of hair behind her ear. "Thank you for paying our way in. It wasn't needed—"

"You're welcome. It was my pleasure."

"Would you like to sit? We can scoot down one."

Emily seemed to become aware of their conversation at that point and turned to face Ian.

"Hi! You can sit next to me." She patted the empty seat beside her.

Ian's gaze rested on his daughter now, and Sarah could see the range of emotion in his eyes. His chest rose visibly and then he released a shuddering breath.

"Well thank you, Emily. I'd like that very much." Ian scooted past Sarah to sit in the empty seat.

As he passed, Sarah couldn't help but check him out. How could she avoid it? Nearly six feet of muscle decked out in traditional Scottish wear? Beneath his black Highland Games shirt was a broad chest she could envision beneath her hands again. Would always fantasize about brushing with her lips.

Ian was all man, and seeing him in that kilt made her

heart do all kinds of funny things.

Where was his entourage of women that all the McLaughlins had seemed to have? Or had that faded over the years?

She glanced over her shoulder. A group of four women who looked to be in their early twenties sat giggling just a few rows behind him now.

All right, maybe the entourage hadn't faded. Her lips quirked and she shook her head in amusement.

Emily seemed to be in true form by chatting non-stop with Ian, but he seemed thrilled by the attention and joined the discussion with animation.

He would gesture to the stage and point out different facts about the dance and Kenzie.

Again, Emily was visibly fascinated. Both by the dancers and Ian.

After the Highland Dancers finished and Kenzie had joined up with them, they all made their way over to the games where Ian and his brothers were set to compete.

They spent a good while watching several games being played. The "weight over the bar" event where men attempted to toss a fifty-six pound weight over a bar with just one hand. Or there was the fascinating "stone put" where the athletes threw a large stone as far as possible.

But what drew the biggest crowd was the caber toss. Women, men and children of all ages lined up to watch the event.

"Look at them all." Kenzie gestured to the athletes set to compete. "You'd swear it was Christmas, they're so excited."

Sarah focused again on all the burly men lined up. Most with large upper bodies and thick calf muscles, no doubt from being constant participants in these types of games.

They were chatting and friendly, but obviously in competitive mode. Almost all wore kilts with some kind of T-shirt—some of the guys had even ripped the sleeves to show off more muscle.

And there was no lack of muscles among them. But then, they'd have to be fairly muscular to lift a nearly twenty-foot pole that weighed close to two hundred pounds.

The three McLaughlin brothers stood together, wide grins on their faces as they chatted and watched the other contestants.

"I'm just saying, I wouldn't kick any of those McLaughlin boys out of my bed for eating crackers."

Kenzie snorted and Sarah turned to stare at the group of women passing by. One had to be close to seventy.

"I see they've still got their fan club," she murmured.

Kenzie rolled her eyes and turned back to the field. "They always will. Not like it goes to their heads or anything."

Sarah didn't miss the sarcasm and laughed softly. Maybe it did go to their heads, but for the most part the McLaughlins were a down-to-earth bunch.

"What did those ladies mean by that, Mom?" Emily

asked. "Toss them out of bed for eating crackers?"

Yikes, she'd heard that too, huh?

"It's just a saying, dear. Oh, look, Ian's about to compete next."

"Oh, really?" Just like that her daughter's attention was diverted. "Come on, Ian, you can do it!"

Ian glanced over at them, his grin expanding as he waved. He blew them a kiss and Emily squealed appropriately.

Sarah couldn't help but shake her head, but when he met her gaze and winked, there were definitely butterflies in her stomach again.

And then Ian turned and went to take his position. Once the long log was hoisted upright, he squatted down and placed his hands low on the log.

Even though she'd seen this done in the handful of games she'd gone to when she was younger, it was different now. More intense and somewhat scarier when the man you loved was participating in the dangerous game.

That last unfiltered thought reverberated through her head and she blinked in dismay.

She loved Ian. Again.

Before she could fully angst over that realization, her attention returned to him as the crowd around them began to scream in encouragement.

Her breath caught as he lifted the long log off the ground.

Emily poked her in the side. "It's like he's carrying a telephone pole. He's really going to throw it?"

"Aye," Kenzie answered for her.

Good thing too, because Sarah couldn't have spoken or looked away from Ian at this moment.

He took a moment to steady the caber against his shoulder, before moving forward quickly. With a roar he tossed it up and outward. The crowd burst into screams as he successfully flipped it end over end.

"That's good, right?" Emily asked, bouncing up and down.

"That's very good," Kenzie agreed with a laugh. "I have very strong brothers."

Instead of returning to the line of competitors, as most of the men before him had done, he strode toward where Sarah, Kenzie and Emily were.

Her heart skipped a beat and as he came closer she could see his eyes bright with excitement and pure male pride.

She wasn't sure what she expected. Maybe a high five to them all, or a quick chat, but it wasn't what he did next.

He leaned over the rope and caught the back of her neck, pulling her forward just enough for his mouth to claim hers.

Hot giddy pleasure rushed through her. That he was so blatantly claiming her as his. And then her eyes snapped open when she realized he'd done this in front of Emily. And Kenzie. And pretty much everyone at the Games.

He pulled away, winked and then returned to the line of

competitors.

"Mom?" Emily's voice rose in disbelief. "Ian just kissed you! Does that mean he's your boyfriend?"

Crap. First Ian had thrown the perfect caber toss, and then thrown *them* both past the point of no return.

∽

WHAT HAD DRIVEN him to do it?

Ian ignored Colin's questioning gaze and kept his attention on Aleck, who was taking his turn in the toss.

Even though he watched his brother, his mind was on Sarah. He'd kissed her in front of everyone. He'd been on a high from such a successful toss. And everything male and primal inside of him had wanted to celebrate it by kissing his woman.

His woman. He'd officially started thinking of Sarah as his again. When? After learning about Emily? No, it had been before that. Even if he'd tried to deny it to himself.

He slid his gaze away from his brother and looked at Sarah again. She was looking right back at him and shaking her head. Her look clearly screaming *what the hell was that?*

The bouncing figure of his daughter caught his attention next. Her face was plastered with a huge smile, and she kept pointing his way. When she noticed him watching, she waved and then gave a thumbs-up.

Apparently Emily approved of the kiss. Which might not be a good thing depending on what decision Sarah chose to make about their future.

He gave her a thumbs-up and a grin, before watching Aleck make a fantastic toss of the caber. Colin went next and did equally well.

The rest of the day passed quickly. After the Parade of Clans he explored the grounds with Emily and Sarah. To his surprise Emily didn't say one word about the kiss—which he assumed meant Sarah had instructed her not to.

"Can I have a sword?" Emily plucked a play sword from a stand at one of the vendors and waved it in the air.

"I'll get it for you."

Sarah arched a brow and leaned toward him. "Spoiling her already, I see."

"Of course," he whispered back, not that Emily would've heard them with the way she was swinging her sword around at an invisible opponent. "I've got a lot of years to make up for."

He'd meant it to be a joke, but the flash of guilt in her eyes made him realize it had been kind of a crap thing to say.

"Sorry."

"No need to apologize. You're right." She gave a brief smile. "And she'll love the sword."

He'd just finished paying for the toy when someone slammed into him from the side.

"Well hello, young lovers." Aleck's booming voice drew several glances from people nearby.

Not about to let go of the friendly attempt to knock him

down, Ian gave him a forceful nudge right back, but his brother didn't move an inch.

Ah, but then he hadn't been caught off guard.

"You did great in the caber toss. All you guys did." Sarah's tone bordered on shy, as if she were a bit embarrassed with the visible shift in her and Ian's relationship.

All because you kissed her. Ah well, it wasn't as if his family hadn't known he and Sarah were heading in that direction, right?

His brother's attention turned to Sarah. "Well thank you, luv. I'm glad you could make it out today. You brought Emily, I trust?"

Ian nodded and gestured to Emily who stood a few feet away, swinging her sword at a metal pole holding up a tent.

"Emily, come meet Aleck."

She lowered the foam sword to her side and bounced over.

"Hi." She lifted her head to stare up at him. "Who are you?"

"I'm your uncle."

Shite!

This time Ian did succeed in shoving his brother hard enough to stumble.

All the while Sarah's mouth hung open a bit and she'd lost a shade of coloring.

"My uncle?" Emily repeated, looking from Aleck to her mom. "No you're not. I don't have any uncles."

Aleck cleared his throat. "Uhmm…"

"You just told a lie, and that's totally not good." She laughed and rolled her eyes, before skipping back to look at the tent full of goodies.

"We've not told the lass yet, you daft idiot."

Aleck's brows rose as he glanced between Ian and Sarah. "You haven't? Any reason why?"

"We wanted to give her an afternoon to get to know you all without any pressure," Sarah explained. "To let her see what the McLaughlins were about."

Aleck grinned. "Beyond whisky and troublemaking you mean?"

"Aye, beyond that." Ian glowered at his brother. "We'll tell her soon, though."

"I was thinking tonight would be good," Sarah murmured.

Ian hadn't been sure she would be ready yet, but one glance in Sarah's eyes showed her resolve.

"Tonight? You're sure?"

"Yes. I'd like to have you back for dinner. Chicken Tikka Masala? It's an Indian dish we love." She lifted a shoulder in a shrug, an impish smile flitting across her face. "Though I cheated and made it in the crock pot this morning since I knew we'd be gone most of the day."

"It sounds amazing, and I would love to come back for dinner."

"Ian's coming for dinner?" Emily bounded up to them

again. "Awesome! My mom's a good cook—you're going to love it."

"I know I will."

"Did someone say Indian food?" Colin joined the group, rubbing his belly. "If so, how do I get an invite?"

"You don't." Ian cast him a warning look.

"And who are you?" Emily asked.

"Are you teasing me already, kid? I'm your—"

Ian drove his fist into his twin's side. "Colin. This is Colin. He's my brother."

"He looks exactly like you. Except you got that funny line running down the side of your face."

"Emily!" Sarah's admonishment was laced with horror.

Unfazed, Ian murmured, "Aye, I do. I was a naughty youth and found myself in more than one fight."

Emily's eyes rounded. "Did you win?"

"Some of them."

"But not that one, huh?"

"Actually, yes, even this one. It's hard to best me." He broke off into a gasp as this time Sarah's elbow drove into his side. When he glanced at her, her gaze clearly said it was time to shut up. "But fighting is bad. Quite bad, actually."

"Well duh. Everyone knows that. Except you, I guess." Her nose crinkled. "I'm sorry you got hurt, though."

"Thank you, Emily. I try not to fight anymore." His gut clenched as a dark memory threatened to surface.

Colin squeezed his shoulder. "Aye, well sometimes

there's no choice, brother."

"You guys all talk funny. I can tell you're related."

As are you, little one. He bit his tongue, knowing that little tidbit would come out tonight with just the three of them. It was bound to be emotional and surely Emily would have a bundle of questions.

Colin seemed to have gotten the hint, just as Aleck had, that Emily hadn't been informed yet.

"We'll let you be then," Aleck said. "But why don't you all join us for lunch tomorrow at the pub? Say, eleven, before it opens?"

"Can I even go to a pub? Is that like a bar?" Emily asked.

Ian laughed, surprised she knew what either was. But then she was ten, maybe he shouldn't have been. "Yes, somewhat. During the day children are more than welcome to come and have lunch."

"Because at night the adults get drunk?" she asked. "That's what Neil would do."

"Emily." Sarah shook her head, and gave their daughter a warning glance. "That's not appropriate."

Neil had been a drunk? Hmm. Ian scowled, and tried to meet Sarah's gaze, but she wouldn't look at him. This guy was sounding more and more like a piece of filth. Hadn't Emily said something about him making Sarah cry too?

"Sorry, Mom." Emily looked at the ground, kicking her sneakered feet into the dirt.

"So lunch at the pub tomorrow?" Ian confirmed. "That'll

work for me."

Sarah nodded. "Us too."

It was an unspoken acknowledgment that by then Emily would understand the McLaughlins were her family.

"Great. Tomorrow at eleven then." Aleck reached down and ruffled Emily's hair. "Nice meeting you, kid."

If Emily was taken aback by Aleck's gesture, her dismay grew visibly when Colin did the same thing and then winked at her.

Then his two brothers disappeared back into the crowd. Who knew where Kenzie had vanished off to?

Emily stared at their retreating backs. "I think I like them. But I'm not sure yet."

Ian laughed and resisted the urge to ruffle her hair too. Something about the two ponytails today made it so tempting.

Glancing at Sarah, he asked, "Are you ready to head out?"

She folded her arms across her chest, looking suddenly nervous. "Don't you want to stay for the closing ceremonies?"

"Generally, I'd say aye. But not today."

The truth felt like a heavy weight upon his shoulders, and more than anything he wanted everything out in the open. He wanted to be back in Sarah's house, just the three of them. Enjoying a lovely dinner, and a much-needed conversation.

Understanding flickered in her gaze, and she nodded. "Then we should go."

"Is it all right if I catch a ride with you? I drove with my brothers."

"Of course." Sarah glanced over at Emily. "Ready, kiddo?"

"Yeah. I wanna go practice my backward handsprings in the front yard again. That's the best yard ever."

They made their way toward the entrance and had just left the fair grounds when someone stepped in front of their path.

Son of a bitch.

Knowing another confrontation was unavoidable, Ian faced it head on.

Chapter Seventeen

"WHAT'S UP, McLAUGHLIN? You compete in the games?"

Ian's demeanor chilled a few dozen degrees. "MacGregor. Aye, I did. Though we're just leaving now."

At the mention of "we" Curt's attention switched to Sarah and Emily. He did a double take when he looked at Emily, before lifting his gaze and arching a brow at Ian.

"I didn't know you had a kid?"

Sarah's indrawn breath was clearly heard, and Ian balled his hands into fists. Anger pounded through his blood and he had to draw in a slow calming breath.

A quick glance showed Emily slipping behind her mom, but clutching her hand. If Curt's words had registered, she didn't show it.

Ian ignored the question. "We're on our way out. If you'll excuse us."

As they moved to walk by, Curt wrapped a beefy hand around Ian's shoulder.

"I need a minute of your time, bro."

Slowly, Ian pried each finger away. "I know what you need, MacGregor, and you should well be aware of my answer by this point."

"Well maybe I don't like your answer."

"We'll meet you at the car, Ian." Sarah's gaze slipped to the ground as she tightened her grip on Emily's hand. "We're near the front of the lot."

Once they were gone, Ian was done holding back. "I told you to leave me the fuck alone."

"There's a few things I realized I forgot to sell you. I've got this big—"

"We're done, got it?" Ian lunged forward and grabbed the other man by the shirt. "You stay the hell away from me and my family."

Curt's lips twisted into a sneer. "I knew that chick wasn't just an acquaintance like you said. And you didn't say nothing about a kid when we were serving time, bro."

"It's not any of your business, and I'm not your bro." Ian shook his head. "I'm done, MacGregor. I've come a long ways from the man I was back then. We're clearly in different worlds now. Go your own path; I'll go mine."

"This is fucking bullshit."

"Do you understand?"

Curt was silent for a moment then grunted. "Yeah. I understand you're stupid as hell to walk away from this kind of deal, but whatever. I'm done with this shit."

"Good." Ian thrust the man away from him, then turned

and walked away.

He joined Sarah and Emily in the car a moment later. She started the car and didn't say a word. Her fingers gripped the steering wheel so hard they were white, and her gaze stayed on the road in front of them as she drove out of the fairgrounds.

He knew he needed to say something, because it was clear she was ill at ease with what had happened. "Sarah?"

She shook her head. "Not now."

Did she intend to ignore him the hour drive home? Shite, it was going to be a long hour. He settled back against the seat and closed his eyes.

How the hell was he going to convince her that Mac-Gregor was a fluke in his life and she wouldn't have to worry about him?

Crap. He heaved a sigh and tried to calm his temper.

"Ian, are you really my dad?"

He stilled at Emily's quiet, serious question. So she'd not only heard Curt's assumption, but had taken the time to process it and consider it.

Trying to be as inconspicuous as possible, he stole a glance toward Sarah for how to proceed. Maybe she would know the best way to stall her until they got home. But she wouldn't look at him.

"Yes, Emily, he is."

Damn. She'd just blurted out the truth without even trying to communicate with him first. He didn't look away from her—couldn't figure out what the hell he could even say next. All he could do was wait for Emily's response.

THERE WAS SILENCE from the back seat and Sarah wondered if she should've just bitten her tongue and waited to tell Emily. But she'd already been so frustrated with what had just happened—that Emily had come face to face with that creepy friend of Ian's—that when her daughter had flat-out asked if Ian was her dad Sarah had just spit out the truth.

The choice hadn't been hard. In the car right away? Or two hours from now over dinner? It wasn't worth trying to stall her just so they could make this conversation go smoothly. Who knew if it would've gone smoothly anyway.

Finally she stole a glance in the rearview mirror to check on her daughter.

Emily was staring at the back of Ian's head, a tiny crinkle between her brows that she knew Emily got from him.

"Really?" she finally asked with suspicion. "Ian's my dad?"

Sarah gave a small nod. "Really."

"You're not lying because I said he was nice?"

Ian laughed at that. "We're telling the truth, Emily. We actually planned to tell you when we got back to the house, but you're so clever you figured it out beforehand."

Sarah gave a small and not so silent harrumph. Figured it out with the help of his no-doubt criminal friend.

SHELLI STEVENS

The quick look Ian gave her was filled with apology.

"So is that why you came to Whidbey Island, Mom? To marry my dad?"

Hearing the hopeful note in her daughter's tone, Sarah tightened her grip on the steering wheel. Crap, this is not the direction she wanted to steer this conversation.

"Honey, it's like I first told you. I came back to work out the details of inheriting Gran's house." Sarah kept her voice patient and light, trying not to betray how deeply this topic shook her. "Ian and I bumped into each other again and have become friends."

"Why didn't you get married when I was born? Why hasn't he come and seen me before?"

Because I never told him about you.

Oh God. Hearing her daughter ask that question was hard enough, but seeing the pain on Ian's face just compounded her guilt.

"I…" She swallowed hard. "Because I…"

"Your mother didn't know if I was ready to be a father," Ian said softly. "She made a decision she felt was best at the time. But the important thing is I'm here now, Emily. And more than anything I want to get to know you and be a part of your life. Are you all right with that?"

Emily was silent for a moment and seemed to be weighing his words.

"Yeah. I'm all right with that. How come I don't look like you though?"

248

"Oh but you do." He turned again and pointed to his eyes. "You see? We both have the McLaughlin green eyes."

"Oh!" Her face lit up and she touched the corner of her eye. "Mom, did you know that? Your eyes are blue, but I have my dad's. That's so cool."

"Aye, it is pretty cool," Ian replied sagely. "And you know, you also remind me of Kenzie when she was a child. You're smaller, but you have some similarities."

"Kenzie." Emily squealed and bounced in the seat. "That means Kenzie is my aunt, huh? She's *awesome*."

"She is awesome. And that also means Colin and Aleck are both your uncles."

"Hey, so that man *wasn't* lying when he said he was my uncle." She sighed. "I owe him an apology, huh, Mom?"

Sarah couldn't help but laugh at the fact her daughter's manners had come back at this moment.

"Yes, you just might, honey."

There was silence again for a few minutes, before Emily let out a squeal of excitement that had obviously been building.

"This is the best summer ever. I found out who my dad is and he's way better than stupid Neil the stepdad."

She felt rather than saw Ian's scrutinizing gaze on her. Emily had certainly dropped enough hints that while Neil had an honorable career in the navy, he wasn't the best husband.

They needed to talk later. They really had so much to

chat about.

⌒

WHEN THEY ARRIVED home, Emily ran outside to practice gymnastics, leaving Sarah alone with Ian.

They lingered in the kitchen where Sarah checked their dinner in the crockpot. Still at least another hour or so.

"I'm sorry. About everything that happened, but especially about this afternoon." He paused, seeming to search for the right words. "Curt MacGregor is someone I met while I served my prison time."

"I gathered."

Just hearing him say the words *prison time* had her stomach dropping to her feet. It was a harsh reminder about the man she'd fallen in love with—or really, the man she'd never stopped loving.

He wasn't perfect—he was at times dangerous as proven by the second-degree assault conviction.

Was he as dangerous as Neil? Maybe not. The closest she'd seen Ian to being violent was when he'd learned about Emily. But even then he'd kept it restrained.

"Curt and I were friends at one point," he admitted, "but it was circumstance-driven. Our lives don't mesh anymore. Our life goals are different. I've asked him to stay away."

"And what *are* your life goals?" She set the lid back on the crockpot and turned to stare at him.

"I want to keep my shop's success. Build upon it." He

sidled closer. "And I want you and Emily beside me. I want the chance to earn your love back, Sarah. You know that I've never stopped loving you."

A declaration of love. He'd given it as a teenager and her heart had swelled like a flooded river. But hearing it now, even though her heart took off at lightning speed, she couldn't quite accept it at face value. How much of this declaration was from the fact that he wanted to be in Emily's life? Why hadn't he said it before he'd known about his daughter? Why now?

"I'm bored." The door slammed just after Emily came inside and uttered one of the most popular tween phrases.

Sarah couldn't have been more grateful for the diversion.

"Go read a book."

"Hmm. No thanks. Can we walk down to town and go out on that dock again?" Emily asked, her gaze darting between Ian and Sarah. Obviously she was oblivious to any tension. "*Please*, I really want to look for starfish."

Sarah shook her head. "Honey, I can't right now. I need to make the saffron rice and heat up the naan."

"I don't mind taking you," Ian offered. "If you'd like to that is, and it's all right with your mother?"

She would have to get used to this, Sarah realized. He was her father. Even if her stomach knotted at the idea of sending Emily off alone with him. It wasn't that she didn't trust him, she just feared the bonding time between the two.

What if he won her over so completely Emily didn't

want to leave the island? To leave him?

You don't even want to leave Ian again. Would you blame her?

"That's fine," she finally answered with a nod. "Behave yourself and listen to Ian, okay?"

Emily made a *woot* of joy and grabbed Ian's hand. "Come on…*Dad.* Oh my gosh that is so cool to say!"

Sarah watched them leave the house, her heart a bit heavier. There was the crunch of tires in the driveway, and then she heard more chatter.

A moment later Kenzie appeared in the doorway.

"Knock, knock. Can I come in?"

"Hey, you. Please do." Sarah waved her inside.

"I just swung by to drop off Emily's sweatshirt. She left it the games while watching me dance."

"Oh, thank you." She took the green Tinker Bell sweatshirt from her friend. "This is one of her favorites and she would've been bummed out. Hey, do you want to stay for dinner? Chicken Tikka Masala."

"No, but oh wow, girl. Save me some leftovers."

Sarah laughed. "You can just stay."

Actually, it would make her feel a bit more at ease having Kenzie here to break up the tension. Her earlier plan of just the three of them sounded a little more intense now.

"Nope. I'm going to let your happy little family eat together and bond." Kenzie's face split into a grin. "I saw the father and daughter walking to the wharf together. Emily was holding his hand and chatting a mile a minute. It was so fantastically adorable."

And to think she'd been worried at one point that Emily might be upset by the discovery Ian was her dad.

Kenzie tilted her head and narrowed her eyes. "And yet, you don't seem too thrilled. What's going on?"

"Nothing. It's just...it's a lot to get used to."

"Really? Just this morning you both were half in love. He kissed you in front of everyone and I figured you guys were on your way to child number two."

Oh that was a possibility with the forgotten condom yesterday, but Sarah wasn't even about to get into that.

"I like Ian—" or love "—but sometimes I wonder if he's the best influence on Emily's life."

"You've got to be kidding me. You've just now decided this?"

"No, I've always known it. I got a little caught up in the physical side of things with Ian. I forgot what held me back all these years. It wasn't just his cheating that night, it was his criminal record." She sighed. "I discovered his felony just as I was about to tell him about Emily, who was one at the time."

"And that's why you didn't tell him?" Disbelief flashed across her friend's face, but underneath it was unease.

Sarah shrugged, feeling the heat of a blush steal up her cheeks. "Not just that. It's Ian overall. He was always getting into trouble. I have to really think about Emily and if it's detrimental to have someone like that in her life on a long-term basis."

Sarah was taken aback by the sudden flash of anger in Kenzie's eyes.

"Someone like that? Do you even know *why* he committed a felony? Why he nearly beat someone to death? Has he told you that yet?"

"No, he didn't say," Sarah admitted. "I'm assuming a bar fight over a girl. An insult. A sneeze he took personally. Does it matter? He nearly beat someone to death."

Kenzie's mouth thinned. "You have no idea."

"Then, please, enlighten me."

"Remember those guys on the wharf the other day?"

"Yes."

"There was one in particular who was harassing me."

"Oh, trust me, I remember." This was it. She was finally getting the scoop on that guy.

"Well, nine years ago outside the pub he tried to rape me," Kenzie explained almost offhandedly.

"What?" Sarah could feel the blood draining from her face.

"Fortunately Ian stumbled upon us. He pulled the guy off me and then proceeded to beat the living daylights out of him," she continued. "Which is what got him arrested and ultimately convicted of second-degree assault."

Kenzie had nearly been raped. The horror of that realization alone left her stomach churning, but knowing Ian had saved her and gone to jail for it...

"But if he was protecting you—"

"Ian nearly killed him. Charles was flown to Harborview in critical condition."

"Well the asshole's obviously fine now," Sarah seethed. "Did he at least get convicted of attempted rape?"

"No. The jury wasn't convinced beyond a reasonable doubt that I wasn't willing. There'd been times I'd been seen flirting with him and we'd left the pub together after an early dinner." She hesitated. "But outside, it moved too fast. He was violent. Scary. And I asked him to stop but he didn't. My fear seemed to get him more excited."

"Oh God, Kenzie, he sounds like a monster. I'm so sorry."

"At the time I had a bit of a reputation as being a little wild. It's a small island socially. The jury knew me—knew my reputation."

"And yet another jury convicted Ian of second-degree assault?" Sarah shook her head, furious now. "Our system is screwed up."

"Ian never had a chance. My attacker was the son of a respected judge on the island. One who made it a personal goal to charge and convict my brother."

No. Oh please no. Sarah's throat grew tight with tears and her heart pounded far too fast in her chest. It made sense with the way the man had seemed to goad Kenzie on the wharf. There'd been a swagger that made Sarah believe he might've gotten away with rape had Ian not found them. And the bastard was still out walking free.

"I-I didn't know. Oh, God, Kenzie. I'm so sorry."

"I am too. But not for myself, for Ian." Kenzie's face pinched and she closed her eyes, shaking her head. "I made stupid choices that day. I nearly invited the damn attack, and ultimately Ian paid the price."

"Don't *ever* say that. I wasn't there, but to say you invited the attack is ridiculous."

Suddenly it flickered through her head. Something Ian had said earlier in the week about how he took the word *no* seriously. She'd half brushed his remark off at the time, but now it made sense.

It was personal. It also explained why he'd insisted on driving her home the other night.

His sister had nearly been raped. His felony was because he'd intervened and taught the guy a lesson.

And she'd been so quick to judge him. So quick to assume the worst about him.

Shame flooded through her and nausea had her stomach churning.

"He doesn't like me to talk about it," Kenzie said quietly. "Doesn't want me to explain why he's considered a felon. He says if people want to be so quick to judge him, then let them. He only spent three months in prison, but he wears the felon label like a scarlet letter on his chest. He doesn't think he's good enough for anyone." She met Sarah's gaze.

"Especially for you."

"Oh God…"

"And that's why it's so hard to hear you judge him. If he hadn't stepped in that night, he never would've gone to prison. He never would've had that felony on his record that you and others are so quick to judge."

"And then this Charles guy would've likely succeeded in raping you." Just saying the words made her almost sick. Brought up a violence in her that probably was very similar to what Ian had experienced.

"What if Ian simply interrupted my fate?" Kenzie's jaw flexed. "Charles is walking the streets free as a bird, and I half suspect he's done this to other women. He knows now he can truly get away with anything."

"I hope not. But I hope you're not implying that you'd be better off having been—"

"Of course I wouldn't be better off, I'd be a mess." She gave a harsh laugh. "Hell, I'm still a bit of a mess. But maybe if I'd had more physical bruises, if somehow it were clearer what had been happening—"

"You're blaming the victim, and if it wasn't yourself you'd be agreeing with me. You had the cards stacked against you, Kenzie. This guy probably found a way to buy that jury. Or they were too blinded by who his dad was."

Kenzie gave a small, sad shake of her head. "It doesn't matter anymore. Really. I only told you so you'd know why Ian went to prison. I'm surprised he didn't tell you."

"No, he didn't." *But then, I never gave him the chance.* She'd been too busy judging him herself, just as Kenzie had pointed out. Ian had probably decided it wasn't worth it to try and explain himself.

"You need to give each other a chance. Get beyond this."

She went silent for a moment and then her head snapped up and she made a small gasp of excitement.

"I have an idea. Since your mom is gone for a few days, why don't I come get Emily after you guys eat dinner and I'll bring her back to my place for a sleepover?"

A night alone with Ian—time to talk about the future— suddenly seemed imperative. And yet...

"I don't know. She's only just met you; it might be too soon for her."

"Yes, well, I'm her aunt. Besides, you know me and trust me. And Emily clearly adores me." Kenzie grinned, her mood obviously lighter now with the change in topic. "Plus I'm her aunt. And she's ten, not five, so I'm sure she'd love a slumber party. Did I mention I'm her aunt?"

Sarah let out a bubble of laughter. "Only about a handful of times."

"Perfect. I'm activating my aunt privileges from this moment forward."

"All right, all right. We'll check with Emily and if she's up for it, she's all yours."

"*Fuck yeah.* I'm going to head out and swing by the grocery store for candy, soda, marshmallows—"

"If you bring my child back to me hyped up on sugar tomorrow, I *will* hurt you." She raised a hand in warning. "And you know you have to watch your mouth around her?"

Kenzie laughed and headed toward the door. "*Heck yeah. Pizza. Chips. Chocolate. One Direction on repeat.*"

"Barf. Have fun with that. You'll win her over in a heart-beat." Sarah turned back to the crockpot to check the food. "See you in a couple of hours."

But even with her friend gone, Sarah couldn't stop thinking about what had nearly happened to Kenzie.

And how Ian had been the avenging angel who'd saved her.

With a heavy heart, she blinked back tears. Oh, God. She had so many wrongs to make right.

Chapter Eighteen

IAN HAD ONLY stepped into fatherhood about twenty-four hours ago, but as he watched Kenzie drive off with his daughter his stomach sank.

"She'll be fine."

Sarah's soft comment had him closing the door and turning to face her.

"I know. Kenzie's amazing with children, and Emily seems quite taken with her already."

Folding her arms over her chest, Sarah gave a small smile. "She is. I thought she might be a little scared to go have a slumber party with someone she just barely knows, but she didn't even let me finish my sentence before running to grab her suitcase." She paused. "I think she loves the idea of having an instant family."

"How long will she have that instant family if you pull her away from us again?"

When she flinched and took a step backward, he knew his words had been far more accusing than intended.

"I haven't made any decisions yet." Her gaze searched

his, and she seemed to want to say more. Or maybe she was waiting for him to say something. "We have a lot to talk about."

"Aye. We do. And it looks like we have the whole night alone."

And yet, talking suddenly sounded like the absolute last thing he wanted to do. He couldn't help but slide a gaze over her and take in the curves of her body beneath the sundress.

After the caber toss—that moment when he'd kissed her in front of everybody—he'd been filled with the need to have her again.

Having a whole night alone. It was something that had never even been an issue. He'd been a single man who'd never dated a woman with a child. Being alone with a woman was never a problem.

And yet now here he was. And this might just be one of the few times he'd have Sarah alone for a while. He didn't want to take their time together for granted.

"Oh no. Ian, you've got that look in your eye."

He took a step toward her. "What look is that, doll?"

"The one that says talking is the last thing on your mind."

"I want to talk. After."

"After what?" She swallowed visibly, but he saw the flare of answering heat in her eyes. "We have sex?"

"Make love. It's never been just sex with you, Sarah." He stopped in front of her and caught her face gently between his hands. "Not then." He pressed a brief kiss against her lips. "And not now."

There was a flash of relief in her eyes before she let out a soft sigh.

"Do you really mean that?"

"I have no reason to lie."

"You have Emily. Maybe you'd say anything to keep us here—"

He crushed the rest of that offensive sentence with a harder kiss. Slipping his tongue out, he teased hers into an equally passionate response.

He lifted his head a moment later. "Does that *feel* like a lie to you?"

She shook her head.

"I've been thinking about it, and if you don't want to move to Whidbey, then I'll accept your decision."

"You will?" Pain flashed in her eyes and her words were choked. "Just like that?"

"Aye." He gave a sage nod. "But you should be warned that I'll plan to move to Virginia as soon as possible."

Her mouth parted. "But...your shop is here. Your family is here."

"I love you, Sarah. I never stopped. And I want to be with you and raise our daughter." His jaw flexed and he let out a shuddering breath, knowing his words were the truth. "If following you to Virginia is what it takes, then aye, I'll do it."

She stared at him a moment longer, before her eyes filled with tears and she blinked them away.

Oh shite. That wasn't good. Now he'd gone and made her cry? "Sarah…"

"You always know exactly what to say," she choked out, before throwing herself into his arms. "You're right, we can talk later. Make love to me, Ian."

His chest swelled with the jolt of pure relief, even as the feel of her body flush against his had need coursing through him.

He caught her hips and kissed her again—more thoroughly this time, as if his leaving or staying would be decided by this moment. The way she clung to him and kissed him back, though, gave him hope.

The last two times he'd made love to her, it had been too quick. He hadn't touched her the way he'd wanted to. Tasted her everywhere he'd wanted to.

Sliding his hand up her back, he found the hidden zipper in the dress and tugged it down. Sarah lifted her head enough to assist him and shrugged out of the sundress.

When the cotton fabric disappeared from her body, a strangled groan escaped him at the sight that was left. No bra, just the sexy curve of her naked breasts and a thin pink thong with flowers on it.

"Ah, you're so lovely."

He watched the shiver take her body at his words. Saw the flare of need in her eyes.

He lifted his hands to cup her breasts, thumbing each dusky peak and watching them tighten in response.

"I love how they do that, doll."

She arched her back, pressing herself firmly into his hands.

"Ian…"

He knew what her soft plea was for, and lowered his mouth to close around one nipple. Her husky moan was all the appreciation he needed.

Lightly, he played with one breast while bathing the nipple of the other with his tongue. Her head fell back against the door and the small moans she made grew in frequency.

His own arousal grew with each flick of his tongue over the soft, textured tip. He sucked harder, grazing with his teeth now.

When her hips slammed into his and she made a sharp cry of need, he knew she was ready for more.

Sliding a hand between them, he moved his palm down her belly to cup the heated mound of flesh between her legs. The discovery of the damp thong had his cock hardening in response.

He traced his fingers back and forth over her sex, wanting to bring her higher on that plateau of desire.

After a moment, she made a cry of frustration and clenched her thighs around his hand. As if to stop the sweet torment. Or maybe it was a plea for more.

"Spread your legs," he ordered softly.

It took a moment before his words even seemed to register, but then she shifted her stance and opened her body to him.

Ian made another slow pass over her mound, before curling two fingers into the panties and tugging them to the side.

He slipped his hand over her naked, heated flesh. His groan mixed with hers at the moisture that he discovered.

Unable to draw out the torment, he slipped a finger deep into her body.

The hot suction of her flesh had him choking out her name.

She curled her hands tighter around his shoulders and moved her head to press her lips against his neck.

While she stoked the fire inside him with seductive nips, he added a second finger inside her and worked them in and out in gentle, but deep strokes.

Her hips rocked against him and the way her sheath suddenly gripped him, he knew she was so close.

Too soon. He wanted to draw it out. Please her other ways.

When he pulled his fingers from her, she cried out in protest.

"Oh don't stop," she whispered raggedly. "Please—"

"I want to go do down on you."

"Oh." She let out a shuddering breath. "When you put it that way…"

He picked her up and carried her across the room, before

setting her on the table they'd so recently dined at.

Her eyes went wide. "Wait, here?"

"Aye." He couldn't help the deep, promising laugh.

Her cheeks reddened with a blush, and he waited for her to protest or push him away. But when he caught the small sides of her thong and tugged them off her hips, her eyes fluttered closed.

Pleasure, or being caught up in the moment, seemed to have won out.

"Your dinner was amazing," he murmured with a lopsided grin, "but I'm in the mind for some dessert."

That earned him a snort of laughter that turned into a gasp when he again pressed a finger back inside.

"Ian…"

"I hope to spend my whole life looking at you. Touching you." He sank down to his knees and pulled her forward, draping her legs over his shoulders. "But I've waited too many years to taste you again."

And with that he was done talking, and ready to claim her in the most intimate way.

He nuzzled her sex, before teasing through the slick folds with his tongue. Tasting her and getting heady on her cries of pleasure. He reached up to cup her arse, squeezing the soft flesh as he teased her clit, stroking the tiny spot over and over, before closing his lips around it and suckling.

"Ian…*oh please*…that feels so good."

Her hips rose and fell against his mouth, as her cries grew

higher and more frantic.

Beneath his hands her arse clenched and she let out a choked gasp. Ian made a murmur of approval and stayed with her as she climaxed—even as his cock strained painfully against his jeans.

When her thighs eased up on their death grip and she went lax, he lowered her back onto the table.

Even with her eyes closed, she fumbled to grab his hand and squeezed it.

"That was incredible." Her soft words were unsteady. "I may need to return the favor."

"I may need to take you up on that. Later." Right now he wanted nothing more than to be inside her. Having her mouth on him, while it would no doubt be fucking amazing, wasn't what he needed right now.

He moved swiftly to his feet, already pulling off his clothes. And then, finally, he remembered the condom in his wallet.

"Let me grab protection."

She caught his hand again, stalling him. "Don't use it on my account."

Her slowly drawled words had him pausing, their meaning sinking in. No protection? And she was okay with the risk? His mind quickened. Did that mean she was staying on the island? Wanted a future with him?

"You're overthinking it." She propped herself up on her elbows and gave a gentle, encouraging smile. "Just make love to me before I take the initiative."

Everything male and primal inside him responded to what was basically a challenge. The image of Sarah pregnant again, and him being there for her this time around—it felt too damn right.

He placed his hands around her tiny waist and lifted her. Her arms and legs wrapped around him as he carried her toward the bedroom.

Theirs mouths fused together in another heated kiss. It distracted him to the point where he stopped to hold her against a wall, needing to just slide inside her for a moment.

Cupping her arse, he supported her weight as he lowered her onto his throbbing cock. Her wet heat welcomed him, and he let out a throaty groan.

"Oh *yes*." Her thighs tightened around his waist and she pressed herself down onto him.

"Ah…." He closed his eyes, rocking up into her in smooth, steady thrusts.

So perfect. Always like coming home when he was with her like this.

They lasted a few minutes taking it slow against the wall, but as his arousal grew more primitive it wasn't enough. He wanted to take her faster, harder.

He moved them again, staying buried deep in her body as he carried her to the bedroom.

"I want to be on top." Her lips pressed against his shoulder. "Please, Ian."

As if he would argue with that? Instead of lying her down as planned, he maneuvered himself onto the bed and reclined, never pulling from her.

Sarah arranged herself on top of him. Her small hands exploring his chest as she began to move on him slowly.

Christ. That felt amazing.

"Ah…just keep doing what you're doing."

"I will." She rode him faster, her nails teasing over his nipples. "You feel so good."

He could get used to this position with her. Watching her breasts sway as she took the initiative, just as she'd promised moments ago.

Unable to completely hand over the reins, he curled his fingers around her waist and thrust up into her.

Her startled gasp was full of pleasure.

"I'm so close."

"Me too." He closed his eyes and plunged again.

She rotated her hips, bringing him deeper and hitting uncharted territory.

"So…close." She threw her head back and let out a series of soft cries.

The spasms of her body around his cock sent him closer to the edge. He took over completely, rolling her back under him and thrusting into her fiercely.

Faster. Until he felt her nails pierce his shoulders and the combination of pain and pleasure hurtled him over the threshold and into oblivion.

"I'm an idiot." Her soft confusing confession a few minutes later brought him down from the nirvana-like high from his release.

"Why?" He lifted himself off her enough to search her gaze, his heart constricting a bit. "Because you slept with me again?"

"No, because I'm a judgmental fool who never questioned why the man I loved might've gone to jail for beating someone up." She touched his cheek and met his gaze.

The man she loved. His heart stuttered at her confession, but she continued talking before he could ask her to repeat it. Just to be sure he wasn't hearing things.

"Kenzie explained everything tonight. I wish you would've told me."

"She did?" Ah, of course she did. Kenzie carried too much guilt and often blamed herself for his prison time. Any chance she had to redeem her big brother, she took it. "I suppose I should've told you, but I've gotten in the habit of being tried and convicted by people. That day in the office, when I told you about my felony, I realized you were likely doing the same."

"I was. And stupid for it. I don't blame you for what you did."

He sighed. "Aye, well the courts did. Colin was just inside the restaurant. I could've summoned him outside to arrest the attacker. Instead I—"

"Instead you acted on emotion. You're a passionate man,

Ian. It's why you responded so strongly when you saw Kenzie being hurt. I don't think it makes you a bad person. More so the opposite. And I've met this guy who attacked her. Excuse my language, but he's a real piece of shit."

"Aye, he is. And unfortunately he's walking free."

"He'll screw up. Karma always catches up with guys like that."

"I sure as hell hope so." He gave a grim shake of his head. He didn't want to think about this. Not now. There was something else looping in his mind.

"Back to something else you said." He pushed a strand of hair back off her forehead. "Did I hear you right when you said you loved me?"

She laughed, her gaze sparkling clearly with the emotion now. It left little doubt he'd heard right.

"You caught that, did you?"

"Caught it. Clung to it. Am so happy that my love isn't one-sided." He cocked his head and pursed his lips, adding lightly, "Though I'm also a bit scandalized by your request that I knock you up again."

Sarah choked on a laugh and slapped at his chest. "I made no such request."

"Mmm hmm. You kind of did, actually, when you told me to take you bareback."

She laughed outright now, a blush stealing her cheeks. "In some ways, you'll never change."

"Do you want me to?"

271

"No. I love you exactly the way you are." She toyed a finger over his chest. "Which is why I don't want to leave Whidbey at the end of the summer."

He stilled, not daring to get his hopes up. "You don't?"

"I don't. I don't want to leave you again, or take Emily from the father and family she's only just discovered."

A shuddering breath of relief escaped him, and he lowered his head to her breasts. He nuzzled the soft flesh there and listened to the rhythmic pounding of her heart.

"I don't think you realize what that means to me." Another thought occurred to him and he lifted his head once more. "So does that mean you'll marry me then?"

A smile flirted around her mouth. "Aye."

He laughed at her attempt at a Scottish accent, even as his heart swelled with love.

"There's no one else for me, Ian. There never has been."

"And Neil? Will he still be a part of Emily's life?" Maybe he shouldn't have asked, especially at this moment, but it was something they would need to discuss.

"No." Her tone dropped and her words chilled. "I made sure in the divorce documents that he has no rights to her. To me."

Good.

There was so much he still didn't know. Should probably know if they were to go forward from here.

"Will you tell me about him? Why you married him?"

"Yes." Pain flickered across her face. "Because my dad set

us up and encouraged us to get together. He was everything my dad wanted for me. A strong military man who would take care of Emily and me. Give us security." She sighed. "I was still so young. So easily influenced. But Neil…was a terrible mistake."

All the little hints she or Emily had dropped in conversations floated back to him. He wanted to know everything. As painful as it might be to hear it.

"Why? What happened?"

She hesitated. "Neil and I spent out honeymoon in a hotel in Tokyo. My dad paid for it. It was the first time we…"

She couldn't finish the words, but Ian heard what she couldn't say. He hated the image of another man touching her. Trying to seduce her. But it was a part of their history. They'd been apart for eleven years, so it was only natural that both of them would've had other lovers. Even if none had ever claimed his heart the way Sarah had.

"And?" he prodded when she didn't go on.

"And it was awful." Her smile was sad, almost bitter. "I knew I didn't love him, and it started to sink in that night that I'd made a mistake. I could only think of you. Any time he tried to touch me, I'd cry." She closed her eyes. "It made him pretty angry. He knew I was thinking about you. Knew I was still in love with Emily's dad."

"And what did he say?"

"He didn't say much. At least not verbally. He let his fists do the talking."

"What the fuck did you just say?" Someone was going to die. Just as soon as he figured out where this son of a bitch was.

Rage spiked inside him and red clouded his vision. Her husband had hit her.

"At the time I thought maybe it was a fluke and he'd just lost his temper with me that night. We didn't try again for months, and I'm pretty sure he found someone else to sleep with. Which I actually was grateful for." She hesitated. "Though now and then he'd want to try again. It was always awful, and so he'd leave me alone for a while. I started saving my money to leave him. My dad had passed away by then and my mom could barely pay the bills. I felt stuck."

Fuck. Dammit, the guilt was squeezing his chest like a wrench.

"But after he came back from his last deployment a year ago he hit me again. And he did it in front of Emily. I moved out that night. It was my breaking point."

"Did he ever hit Emily?"

"No. I would've killed him."

His chest couldn't seem to untighten from the mass of knots it'd become. "But he hit you."

"Not often, but yes. I'm not proud that I stayed as long as I did—"

"Fucking hell. I should've been there—"

"Don't even make this your fault. Don't shoulder this blame. You didn't know. You couldn't have known. I should've never married him in the first place."

"I suppose there's a lot of things we should've done, or shouldn't have done." He sighed and shook his head. "We made some wrong turns in life, and I can only think that this all would've been avoided if I hadn't made that huge fucking mistake with Hailey."

"Listen to me, Ian. I forgive you for it." She met his gaze squarely. There was only a hint of sadness there, but the dominant emotion was sincerity. "I think I did years ago, honestly. We were both so damn young and neither of us made the best choices. I'm not without guilt. I said horrible things to you that were only driven from a broken heart. I didn't mean them."

She forgave him for that night. Amazing. How was he blessed with such an amazing woman?

"Sarah." He kissed her gently. "I should've tried harder to keep you and known your words were empty. I should've tried to find you in Japan."

"As much as you broke my heart that day, I broke yours as well."

Aye. She had. And yet he would never blame her for it.

"Pain can make us do stupid things." She bit her lip and shook her head. "I hope some day you'll be able to forgive me for not telling you about Emily."

"I don't blame you. I might've done the same. You didn't know the details of my conviction, and you had to think of Emily. We played the hand life dealt us."

She kissed his chest and made a soft sigh. "I think Gran left me the house to give us a bit of a push. Thanks to her, we have a new hand. A fresh start."

"And I intend to play that hand like a bitch and win big," he growled and lowered his head to kiss the tip of one breast again.

Her laugh turned into a moan, and beneath his weight she squirmed. Her legs opening to him again.

"I've already won big," she murmured. "I have you. I love you so much."

His heart swelled. "I love you more."

"Not possible."

He caught her hands and slid them above her head, pinning them there. Using his knees, he pushed her thighs apart and then sank back into her slick body again.

"I guess I'll just have to prove it."

"Yes." Her eyes closed and she sighed with pleasure. "I guess so."

Chapter Nineteen

MUSIC PIPED THROUGH the speakers of McLaughlin's Pub. The pub was closed, but you wouldn't know it by the laughter and tears flowing in the establishment.

Sarah watched as Kenzie attempted to teach Emily some of the dance moves for Highland Dancing.

The announcement that she and Emily were staying on the island had been greeted with cheers, tears and toasts. Even more frenzy-inducing news was that Sarah and Ian were going to get married.

"Even your mom's dancing," Ian murmured next to her. "I don't think I've ever seen her dance."

"She's not bad, huh?" Sarah smiled and snuggled closer beneath her future husband's arm.

He glanced down at her and smiled. The intimacy and love that shone in his eyes made her heart skip.

When was the last time she'd been this happy? Felt so completely full and perfect? Emily had brought a love and enrichment into her life she'd never known was possible. But Ian had been the missing puzzle piece that by chance had never worked before.

"Hi, Mom. Hi, *Dad*—oh it never gets old!" Emily came bouncing over, eyes twinkling.

The slumber party with Kenzie had been *amazing*, from what Emily had said. Kenzie had taken her auntie liberties to the extreme. Emily wore a sparkly brand-new dress loaded with glittery happy faces and peace signs, black boots with buckles, and her hair was braided into several intricate-looking twists and loops.

"Hello, my adorable daughter." Ian reached out and snagged his daughter, tickling her on the side.

Emily squealed with delight and hugged Ian. "Do I get to be a flower girl in your wedding? Or am I too old? 'Cause if I'm too old, I should at least get to be a bridesmaid."

Sarah laughed, her heart so full of happiness and love, it didn't feel as if her chest could contain it.

"You can be whatever you want to be, honey."

Emily narrowed her eyes, the gesture so like her dad, and then nodded.

"Bridesmaid. That flower girl thing is for little kids. And I'm a tween."

And with another whoop of excitement, she was off again to rejoin Kenzie on the dance floor.

"Food's here."

Aleck and Colin appeared with plates full of fries, shepherd's pies, fried fish, and more food than anyone could eat in a day—let alone the next hour before the pub was set to open to the public.

Sarah watched as everyone gathered around the two tables they'd pulled together. Hands blurred in a flash as people began to divide and conquer the food.

Eleven years later, and she was exactly where she was meant to be. They'd come full circle.

A soft, content sigh escaped her.

Ian squeezed her shoulder and she glanced up at him. The same look that must've been in her eyes was in his. So much love. So much happiness.

"I love you," he murmured.

"I love you more." She lifted her head and met the kiss he was already leaning down to take.

To quote their daughter, *it never got old…*

PARKING HER CAR outside the pub, she swallowed hard and wondered if she were crazy.

You could just leave. You don't need to do this.

No. She couldn't.

Pushing open her door, she strode across the parking lot and headed to the front door of McLaughlin's Pub.

She hesitated, just for a moment. One foot turned back toward her car, the temptation to just turn and drive away still so strong.

No. They deserved to know. After smoothing a hand down her scrubs and pushing back the fatigue from working an overnight shift, she opened the door.

It took a moment for her gaze to adjust to the dim lighting and to locate the group inside.

"I'm sorry, but we're not yet open," a male voice called out.

"No wait."

She recognized Ian McLaughlin as he stood from the table.

"Hailey?"

She nodded, the lump in her throat so massive she couldn't breathe past it.

"Get out." Another chair scraped on the floor, and her startled gaze darted to Ian's twin brother, Colin, as he strode quickly toward her. "You have no business here."

Before he could reach her, Sarah was at his side, pulling him back.

"It's fine, Colin. Please, sit down."

For a moment, Colin's gaze locked on Hailey's and the blazing resentment in them had her flinching. She expected it from Ian and Sarah, but hadn't prepared herself to see it from a family member. How naïve of her.

"Is there something we can help you with?" Sarah's tone, though polite, held a thread of tension.

This was the Sarah she remembered. Patient and nice, even when she had every reason to hate her. An ache bloomed in her heart and not for the first time she missed the friendship with Sarah she'd destroyed.

"Hello, Sarah. Ian." Hailey thrust her hands into the pockets of her scrubs and forced a slight smile. "Could we talk for a moment? Privately?" She appeared as if she wanted to turn tail and run. "Maybe step outside?"

Sarah glanced at Ian, and they seemed to communicate silently before she nodded.

"All right."

Hailey turned and walked back out of the pub, knowing the other two would follow her.

The parking lot was deserted and offered them the privacy she needed.

She turned to face them and her heart sank. There was so much regret and pain on Ian's face. His gaze wouldn't meet hers as his arm stayed securely around Sarah's waist.

They were together again. As they always should've been. She'd heard the rumors that Sarah had returned, and then that she and Ian were involved again. But it was only when she'd learned the two had a daughter that Hailey knew she had to come forward.

"Hailey," Sarah began, discomfort clear in her voice. "We don't really need to do this. Ian and I are trying to forgive and forget what happened that night—"

"That's just it. You don't *know* what happened that night." Hailey drew in a shuddering breath, and glanced at Ian. "Neither of you do."

Sarah shook her head.

"You mean I was just too drunk to remember?" Ian said

flatly. "I have a good guess. There's no need to go into details—"

"There is, actually." Hailey closed her eyes briefly. "I should've done this years ago."

"Done what?" Sarah's tone shifted into unease.

No turning back now. They already despised her. While what she was about to tell them may not make things easier, it would shift the hurt. Shift the betrayal. And they deserved to know the truth.

Hailey took a deep breath and forced herself to continue. "Back in high school, I was in a really bad place. You probably heard the rumors. My parents were crackheads and dirt poor. More than once CPS got involved, and there was a real danger of my younger brother and I being taken away. Separated."

It was hard to talk about it, because it seemed a lifetime ago. There was so much shame associated with those years.

"I heard the rumors," Sarah admitted. "Though I wasn't sure if they were true. You kept that part of your life pretty private."

She'd had to.

"Things got even worse my senior year," she went on. "Mom was late on bills and really hurting for money, and the ways she was talking about earning it…weren't good." Hailey drew in a ragged breath, hesitated, and then lifted her gaze to meet Sarah's dead on. "So when your dad approached me and offered me five hundred dollars to make it look like I slept with Ian, I said yes."

No one said anything for a moment, but the small, choked gasp came from Sarah. Ian caught her as her knees seemed to give out.

"My dad?" Sarah repeated, shaking her head. "He would never…"

Her words drifted off, and Hailey could see the moment Sarah gave up on that argument. The moment she decided her dad *would* have done that.

Ian seemed a bit less convinced.

"I may not remember much about that night, but I remember you climbing into bed with me. Why would I remember that if we didn't have sex?"

"I kept plowing you with drinks, Ian. To make it look like you were just wasted." Oh crap it was so hard to admit this. "But I slipped something like a roofie into your drink. Your dad suggested it, Sarah, and with my parents being who they were, it wasn't hard to get one."

"The fuck you did."

Despite his roar of protest, there was realization in Ian's eyes now. She could see the belief take over the shock, even as he denied it.

"It's why you don't remember what happened that night. Why it was so easy to convince everyone—including you—that we'd slept together." She was going to be sick. Saying all this, confessing to the horrible sin she'd committed against them.

She was a nurse; she saved lives now. But what she'd done that night…

"Fuck." Ian pulled Sarah closer to him. "I know your dad hated me, but I never could've imagined him doing this."

"Neither could I." Her voice broke and she stared up at Ian. "I'm surprised, and yet I'm not. Lately I'm learning my dad wasn't the man I thought he was."

"Ah, Sarah." Ian pulled her into his arms and held her.

"Again, I should've never been so quick to assume," Sarah whispered. "That morning when I found you, my gut screamed you'd never do that to me, but logically…"

"Hell, I was convinced I'd slept with her."

"You didn't. Oh my God, you didn't." There was joy in Sarah's teary laugh now.

Ian joined in, his laughter filled with amazement. "I loved you too much. It never made sense. I still love you so much."

Uncomfortable now and feeling intrusive on their moment, especially when they kissed, Hailey wanted to just back away, and leave them to wade through the discovery.

But Sarah pulled away from Ian suddenly to look at her, blushing as she seemed to remember where they were.

"Thank you, Hailey. I know you didn't have to tell us."

"Of course I did." Her mouth curled into a bitter smile. "I've regretted my choice every day since. I'm not proud of what I did. I'm not going to make this about me and say I mourned our loss of friendship, Sarah. That's a given." Tears burned at the back of her eyes, but she struggled to keep them back. "I regretted ruining your relationship most of all. And when I heard you were back and that you and Ian had a child, I knew I had to come clean."

"Thank you." Ian gave a slight nod, even as he still wouldn't look her in the eye.

She understood. It was a break in trust. A lot to take in. There was so much emotion flowing between them at that moment.

Hailey nodded and pulled her keys from her shoulder bag. "I'll leave now. Good luck in life."

She turned and walked away, climbing into her car a moment later. But with her hands shaking so hard she knew it would be another couple of minutes before she should drive.

Ian and Sarah walked back to the pub, arms around each other and talking with heads together before they disappeared inside.

She'd done the right thing. She knew she had. Maybe Sarah had heard some things about her dad that were upsetting, but she now knew Ian was innocent. And that had been Hailey's goal.

Fumbling to put the keys in the ignition, she paused when the door to the pub again swung open.

Her chest went tight at the sight of Colin McLaughlin, large and intimidating with his glower, striding toward her.

Her windows were already open due to the heat, and he

curled large hands around the frame and dipped his head down to look at her.

"Let me give you some advice, Hailey." His voice was ice and it worked in chilling her to the bone.

"Stay away from them," he continued. "You're nothing but trouble and you've got no place in their lives. Not Sarah's, Emily's, or any of the McLaughlins'."

Her stomach clenched at the verbal kick. He fit well into his law enforcement image. Writing her off as trouble, no doubt because of who her family had been. Even if she hadn't seen them in years.

"Well aren't you the protective guy in the family," she couldn't help but reply tightly past the hurt.

"Aye. I sure as hell am. But you don't really want to find out through trial and error."

She gave a laugh of disbelief, and knew she should've bitten her tongue as she muttered a snarky, "You sure you're not overcompensating for something by wearing that badge, Sheriff?"

His nostrils flared. "Excuse me?"

She turned her gaze away from his unsettling stare. "I'll stay away, Colin. You don't need to worry about me."

No one had in years anyway. She did fine on her own, and would continue to do so.

Still, as she backed out of the parking lot, she couldn't help but lift her gaze to the rearview.

Colin hadn't moved, but watched after her with an even

deeper scowl still.

Maybe Mother Nature had to be somewhat kind and make him sexy, because clearly the man was a judgmental asshole. And actually kind of mean.

And he called *her* trouble?

She grunted and turned her gaze back to the road.

Stay away from the McLaughlins? No problem.

The End

The McLaughlins

Available now at your favorite online retailer!

About the Author

Shelli is a New York Times and USA Today Bestselling Author who read her first romance novel when she snatched it off her mother's bookshelf at the age of eleven. One taste and she was forever hooked. It wasn't until many years later that she decided to pursue writing stories of her own. By then she acknowledged the voices in her head didn't make her crazy, they made her a writer.

Shelli is a true pluviophile (lover of rain) and currently lives in the Pacific Northwest with her husband and two daughters. She writes various genres of romance, but is most known for her contemporary series such as Holding Out for a Hero, The McLaughlins, and A is for Alpha. She's a compulsive volunteer, and has been known to spontaneously burst into song.

Visit her website at ShelliStevens.com

Thank you for reading

One More Round

If you enjoyed this book, you can find more from all our great authors at TulePublishing.com, or from your favorite online retailer.

Made in the USA
Columbia, SC
30 September 2021

46013668R00178